REMINISCENCES OF A BACHELOR

Reminiscences of a Bachelor

by

J. Sheridan Le Fanu

Swan River Press
Dublin, Ireland
MMXXII

Reminiscences of a Bachelor
by J. Sheridan Le Fanu

Published by
Swan River Press
Dublin, Ireland
in February MMXXII

www.swanriverpress.ie
brian@swanriverpress.ie

This edition © Swan River Press
"Introduction" © Matthew Holness
"From an Ancient, Leathern Armchair"
and "Some Notes on 'The Watcher' "
© Jim Rockhill & Brian J. Showers

Cover design by Meggan Kehrli
from "The Bachelor" (2014) by Paul Lowe

Set in Garamond by Ken Mackenzie

Paperback Edition
ISBN 978-1-78380-759-8

Swan River Press published
a limited hardback edition of
Reminiscences of a Bachelor
in December 2014.

Contents

Introduction

Today, Joseph Sheridan Le Fanu's classic status rests largely upon his supernatural output and the gothic mystery novel *Uncle Silas* (both arguably the greatest works in their respective fields). His remaining mystery novels, of which there are many, are either out of print or poorly served in cheap editions, far removed from shelves housing almost every "sensation" novel ever penned by Wilkie Collins.

Despite his revered reputation and influence on esteemed writers such as M.R. James and James Joyce no less, Le Fanu is still not a household name. His vast output of gothic suspense fiction languishes in relative obscurity, just as "The Fatal Bride" has done, quietly waiting for an opportunity for reappraisal.

Le Fanu was hugely successful in his day, of course. He wrote ghost stories, mystery novels, and occasionally ghost stories within mystery novels, seeing no real need to distinguish one fictional "reality" from another.

There's a reason for this.

Though he is regarded by many as the true godfather of the classic ghost story, Le Fanu is not, despite frequent assumptions, a practitioner of the M.R. James school of cosy, "pleasing terror". James learned much from Le Fanu, and freely admitted so. The gradual emergence of Le Fanu's ghosts, paced for optimum, cumulative effect, and their relentless taking over of the victim's world are structural techniques James admired greatly and subsequently perfected himself.

But Le Fanu's tales possess a unique, overwhelming darkness entirely their own. The tone is understated; sombre. Unlike James, Le Fanu concentrates on showing the psychological effect of a haunting upon the haunted. He specialises in depicting the internal and external deterioration of his characters; the nervous anxiety, depression, and suicidal impulses brought about by their lonely, irrational predicaments.

Le Fanu's stories are by turns terrifying, bleak, and desperately sad. They capture the unbearable isolation of the victimised, and the cruel self-castigation of the tortured mind.

Whether or not the clinical accuracy of Le Fanu's depiction of psychological disorders derived from his wife's crippling anxiety or his own private complaints cannot be claimed with certainty. However, it is evident that he had first-hand knowledge of such maladies. The character of Charles Fairfield in *The Wyvern Mystery* (itself containing interesting parallels with both "The Watcher" and "The Fatal Bride") is one of the most chillingly convincing portrayals of guilt-induced paranoia ever committed to prose.

Yet throughout Le Fanu's fiction, and his ghost stories in particular, explanations are generally left open to interpretation. He peppers his tales with experts: religious, medical, none of whom prove any use whatsoever to his doomed protagonists. And whether the ghosts he depicts are ultimately real or imagined is arguably irrelevant. Le Fanu's Swedenborgian entities operate within, and as part of, our own realm; inhabiting and influencing the world of human enterprise, conflict, and exploitation. The hauntings are frequently forms of self-punishment. Le Fanu's ghosts emerge just as readily from the victim's own suppression of a private impulse as they do from any supernatural plane. His tormented victims, and there are many, might be blameless or blameworthy. Or both. Unresolved internal conflicts abound. Crippling self-denial. Private guilt.

There is no finer example of this, perhaps, than the two "Reminiscences of a Bachelor" you are about to read. Presented here for the first time in their original form, both have very different histories. One is a ghost story, the other a gothic mystery. The former, "The Watcher", was originally published in the November 1847 edition of the *Dublin University Magazine* and became one of Le Fanu's most celebrated tales of the supernatural. The second, "The Fatal Bride", appeared two months later in the same publication and has not been reprinted until now.

Both tales are classic Le Fanu. Taken together, they showcase the two "opposing" branches of his fiction while exploring similar themes. Significantly, both stories inhabit the same reality. They take place in the same streets and share the same narrator; the unnamed "Bachelor", who plays a minor role in each tale.

In "The Watcher", his brief involvement is confined to an evening walk with Captain Barton, a role that was given to "Norcott" in the 1851 version of the tale. In this earlier form, the Bachelor and a mutual acquaintance accompany Barton down to the House of Commons, witnessing not only the debilitating effects of the haunting upon their companion, but also the first physical manifestation of the ghost itself.

In "The Fatal Bride", however, the Bachelor's involvement in the narrative increases, as does his own significance as a character. Determined to relate only "faithful narratives of fact" while "maintaining my incognito", the Bachelor himself is unnamed, unknown and possibly unreliable. Like the protagonists in the stories he relates, his behaviour is secretive and occasionally clandestine. He claims to be "as peaceable a fellow as any among her majesty's liege subjects" while later "thread[ing] the narrow alleys and back lanes with a careless sort of swagger, and a pugnacious disposition", all the while drunk and armed with a sword. It's telling that his one moment of active participation in the story's events is an intrusion made while inebriated and free from personal inhibition. Meanwhile, his initial impression of the "Fatal Bride" herself, Mary Chadleigh, is an ostensibly chaste, if somewhat romantic, study:

> I observed her with the deep and silent pleasure with which beauty of the highest order may be contemplated, without the smallest danger to the heart . . .

Yet later he admits that "I never saw, at least in my young days, a pretty girl, without feeling a disposition to fight with somebody". Well, love's one thing. Lust quite another.

The question of marriage in both these stories forces the issue, somewhat. In "The Watcher", the haunting of Captain Barton commences the moment he becomes engaged to Miss Montague. Meanwhile, in "The Fatal Bride", Sir Arthur Chadleigh forbids Captain Jennings from courting his daughter largely for the lack of financial gain he will receive upon them marrying, but also, we suspect, in vicarious revenge for his own wife's affair and subsequent hold over their daughter's affections. Mary is thus regarded as mere property in Sir Arthur's case, and a means of sexual gratification for Jennings.

Significantly, there is one character in the story acknowledged openly as a person of genuine honour and integrity. Doctor Robertson, who risks his own livelihood and reputation to aid the unfortunate Mary, stands out starkly from this controlling environment of oppressive male rivalry and sexual aggression. Which leaves our humble Bachelor where exactly? To the "darkness and repose to which time is hurrying us all"? Or, to pin his own words down more precisely, with an awareness that "the nature of the beast pervades us all"?

It's our own identification with the Bachelor and implied acquiescence in the events depicted that disturbs here in much the same way as Le Fanu's handling of the supernatural does. The subversive qualities inherent in the psychological complexities of Le Fanu's tales get right under our skin. His stories feel far more threatening and disruptive than their age and reader expectation might suggest.

Ultimately Le Fanu's ghosts and mysteries are of human origin. Which is why there is so much more to discover and explore in his neglected work. The recurrence of plot situations, characters, and themes don't feel to me like a paucity of ideas. Rather, they represent Le Fanu's compulsive reworking of private obsessions that quietly illuminate dark realities hiding within us all.

Because Le Fanu never quite states what is really going on—maybe that's why his books proved popular in an age of staunch social and religious conservatism. They allowed the repressed reader room enough to squirm.

Deeper appreciation of Le Fanu's vision emerges, like his ghosts, from what the stories awaken in the dark recesses of our own minds. Secrets that we, like the doomed characters in his tales, may very well take to our grave.

Matthew Holness
Norwich, Norfolk
November 2014

Prologue

I am now an old man, and, what is perhaps less excusable, an old bachelor too; and yet, sir, I am not a bachelor of *malice prepense*—I am no profane railer against wedlock. I would not, for my grandmother's enamel *bonbonniere*, which catches my eye this moment, nor for my honoured uncle's silver-mounted and inlaid steel barrels—both of them family reliques dear in their own several ways—that your fair readers should set me down as guilty of premeditated and deliberate celibacy. No such thing. I have more than once narrowly escaped—I should say *missed*—the fate-matrimonial, and that by pure accident—by no cowardice or perfidy of mine. No; my tendencies were all conjugal—my blessedness, however, has been single; and so far am I from thanking my stars, or taking merit to myself for this state of things, that, sooth to say, even the seventy-and-five winters and summers that have bleached and baked me in succession, still find me, now and then, sighing over the tender recollections and bitter disappointments, which are now for me, the sad and only reliques of the romance of early days.

But though I have had my passages of love, as well as those of the sterner passions, in my day; and though I sometimes take a whim to rummage among old trinkets, lockets, and likenesses, each of them to me a little history in itself, yet I would not have you suppose me a superannuated sentimentalist either. No, sir. I have my tender, and, jesting aside, my melancholy retrospections; but I have also my pleasant, and, even at this time of day, my exciting recollections, too. I would be almost ashamed to tell you how often it comes to pass, that, my solitary pint of old port finished, I find myself sunk in my comfortable, ancient, leathern chair, gazing between my knees into the clear red embers, between which and me are rising and floating, like mystic shapes from an enchanted caldron, the forms and faces long lost to life, which have mingled in the mazes of early adventure; and some of whom have left upon my time-chilled heart, traces that eternity itself, mayhap, will fail to obliterate.

Thus it is, that in long winter's evenings, as I sit alone and musing, memory calls up, with chastened colouring and softened outline, the chequered past before me. Passive, as though the pageant were the creation of some Prospero, and I his wondering visitor, I sit by and see, while memory and association crowd my vision with their filmy troops, fragments of old adventure, and glimpses of thrilling scenes, with all their actors duly accoutred, and looking just as they did—how many years ago! The light-hearted and the moody—the loved and the worthless—the prosperous and the ruined—the changed, and the dead and gone—all, in defiance of time and death, take their old places, and wear their old looks and liveries, as they drift by me in sad and wayward procession. Leaving these recollections to themselves, to rise, and shift, and unroll before my listless gaze, as chance, or some unknown law of suggestion wills it, it often happens that strange occurrences, and striking and mournful histories, which had passed from my ordinary remembrances, are thrown up again, like long-buried treasures from the restless sea, and startle me almost with the vividness of novelty.

It may be, that feeling, in most of these stories, that interest which attaches to an acquaintance with the individuals who have taken a part in them, I am unduly predisposed to exaggerate the degree of favour with which an ordinary reader may be presumed to regard them. Incidents well worth recording, as having happened to my lord or lady this, that, or t'other, may yet prove dull enough in the abstract, and unsupported by the borrowed importance of the aforesaid distinguished titles. But whatever interest I might have thrown over these pages, by particularising individuals, and publishing real names, I feel bound—in some cases by humanity, in others by honour, but in *all* effectually—to forego. A *chronique scandaleuse* is not quite the thing for your respectable pages, nor, independently of other and higher considerations, are the tease and worry to which such authorship would expose your humble servant, quite the thing for an easy old bachelor, who has not handled a pistol in anger for full five-and-thirty years, who wishes well to all mankind, and hates trouble, almost as much as law or bloodshed.

The tales I send you, therefore, shall not record the *names* of those whose acts, follies, or sufferings, they recite. In all other respects they shall be faithful narratives of fact—in this alone fictitious. They may prove wondrous dull, as old men's stories sometimes do. Of their merits, I am, for every reason, the worst possible judge. Decide, then, yourself—put them into your Magazine or into your fire, just as your critical acumen shall determine. As for me, I prize my snug obscurity too justly to aspire to literary honours, or to participate in literary resentments. Blot, burn, or print, just as you please; I have nothing of the *genus irritabile*, except, perhaps, some symptoms of the *cacoëthes scribendi* about me.

The Watcher

From the Reminiscences of a Bachelor

It is now more than fifty years since the occurrences which I am about to relate caused a strange sensation in the gay society of Dublin. The fashionable world, however, is no recorder of traditions—the memory of selfishness seldom reaches far—and the events which occasionally disturb the polite monotony of its pleasant and heartless progress, however stamped with the characters of misery and horror, scarcely ever outlive the gossip of a season; and, except perhaps in the remembrance of a few more directly interested in the consequences of the catastrophe, are in a little time lost to the recollection of all. The appetite for scandal, or for horror, has been sated—the incident can yield no more of interest or of novelty—curiosity, frustrated by impenetrable mystery, gives over the pursuit in despair—the tale has ceased to be new, grows stale and flat—and so, in a few years, inquiry subsides into indifference, and all is forgotten.

I was a young man at the time, and intimately acquainted with some of the actors in this strange tale; the impression which its incidents made upon me, therefore, were deep and lasting. I shall now endeavour, with fulness and precision, to relate them all, combining, of course, in the narrative, whatever I have learned from various sources, tending, however imperfectly, to illuminate the darkness which involves its progress and termination.

Somewhere about the year 1794, the younger brother of a certain baronet, whom I shall call Sir James Barton, returned to Dublin. He had served in the navy with some distinction, having commanded one of his majesty's frigates during the greater part of the American war. Captain Barton was now apparently some two or three-and-forty years of age. He was an intelligent and agreeable companion, when he pleased it, though generally reserved, and occasionally even moody. In society, however, he deported himself as a man of the world, and a gentleman. He had not contracted any of the noisy brusqueness sometimes acquired at sea; on the contrary, his manners were remarkably easy, quiet, and even polished. He was in person about the middle size, and somewhat strongly formed—his countenance was marked with the lines of thought, and on the whole wore an expression of gravity and even of melancholy; being however, as we have said, a man of perfect breeding, as well as of affluent circumstances and good family, he had, of course, ready access to the best society of the metropolis, without the necessity of any other credentials. In his personal habits Mr. Barton was unexpensive. He occupied lodgings in one of the *then* fashionable streets in the south side of the town— kept but one horse and one servant—and though a reputed free-thinker, yet lived an orderly and moral life— indulging neither in gaming, drinking, nor any other vicious pursuit—living very much to himself, without forming any intimacies, or choosing any companions, and appearing to mix in gay society rather for the sake of its bustle and distraction, than for any opportunities which it offered of interchanging either thoughts or feelings with its votaries. Barton was therefore pronounced a saving, prudent, unsocial sort of a fellow, who bid fair to maintain his celibacy alike against stratagem and assault, and was likely to live to a good old age, die rich, and leave his money to an hospital.

It was soon apparent, however, that the nature of Mr. Barton's plans had been totally misconceived. A young lady, whom we shall call Miss Montague, was at this time introduced into the gay world of Dublin, by her aunt, the Dowager Lady L——. Miss Montague was decidedly pretty and accomplished, and having some natural cleverness, and a great deal of gaiety, became for a while a reigning toast. Her popularity, however, gained her, for a time, nothing more than that unsubstantial admiration which, however pleasant as an incense to vanity, is by no means necessarily antecedent to matrimony—for, unhappily for the young lady in question, it was an understood thing, that beyond her personal attractions, she had no kind of earthly provision. Such being the state of affairs, it will readily be believed that no little surprise was consequent upon the appearance of Captain Barton as the avowed lover of the penniless Miss Montague.

His suit prospered, as might have been expected, and in a short time it was confidentially communicated by old Lady L—— to each of her hundred-and-fifty particular friends in succession, that Captain Barton had actually tendered proposals of marriage, with her approbation, to her niece, Miss Montague, who had, moreover, accepted the offer of his hand, conditionally upon the consent of her father, who was then upon his homeward voyage from India, and expected in two or three months at furthest. About this consent there could be no doubt—the delay, therefore, was one merely of form—they were looked upon as absolutely engaged, and Lady L——, with a rigour of old-fashioned decorum with which her niece would, no doubt, gladly have dispensed, withdrew her thenceforward from all further participation in the gaieties of the town. Captain Barton was a constant visitor, as well as a frequent guest at the house, and was permitted all the privileges of intimacy which a betrothed suitor is usually accorded. Such was the relation of parties, when the mysterious circumstances which darken this narrative with inexplicable melancholy, first began to unfold themselves.

Lady L—— resided in a handsome mansion at the north side of Dublin, and Captain Barton's lodgings, as we have already said, were situated at the south. The distance intervening was considerable, and it was Captain Barton's habit generally to walk home without an attendant, as often as he passed the evening with the old lady and her fair charge. His shortest way in such nocturnal walks lay, for a considerable space, through a line of street which had as yet been merely laid out, and little more than the foundations of the houses constructed. One night, shortly after his engagement with Miss Montague had commenced, he happened to remain unusually late, in company only with her and Lady L——. The conversation had turned upon the evidences of revelation, which he had disputed with the callous scepticism of a confirmed infidel. What were called "French principles," had in those days found their way a good deal into fashionable society, especially that portion of it which professed allegiance to Whiggism, and neither the old lady nor her charge were so perfectly free from the taint, as to look upon Mr. Barton's views as any serious objection to the proposed union. The discussion had degenerated into one upon the supernatural and the marvellous, in which he had pursued precisely the same line of argument and ridicule. In all this, it is but truth to state, Captain Barton was guilty of no affectation—the doctrines upon which he insisted, were, in reality, but too truly the basis of his own fixed belief, if so it might be called; and perhaps not the least strange of the many strange circumstances connected with this narrative, was the fact, that the subject of the fearful influences we are about to describe, was himself, from the deliberate conviction of years, an utter disbeliever in what are usually termed preternatural agencies.

It was considerably past midnight when Mr. Barton took his leave, and set out upon his solitary walk homeward. He had now reached the lonely road, with its unfinished dwarf walls tracing the foundations of the projected rows of houses on either side—the moon was shining mistily, and its imperfect light made the road he trod but additionally dreary—that utter silence which has in it something indefinably exciting, reigned there, and made the sound of his steps, which alone broke it, unnaturally loud and distinct. He had proceeded thus some way, when he on a sudden heard other footfalls, pattering at a measured pace, and, as it seemed, about two score steps behind him. The suspicion of being dogged is at all times unpleasant; it is, however, especially so in a spot so desolate and lonely; and this suspicion became so strong in the mind of Captain Barton, that he abruptly turned about to confront his pursuers, but, though there was quite sufficient moonlight to disclose any object upon the road he had traversed, no form of any kind was visible there. The steps he had heard could not have been the reverberation of his own, for he stamped his foot upon the ground, and walked briskly up and down, in the vain attempt to awake an echo; though by no means a fanciful person, therefore he was at last fain to charge the sounds upon his imagination, and treat them as an illusion. Thus satisfying himself, he resumed his walk, and before he had proceeded a dozen paces, the mysterious footfalls were again audible from behind, and this time, as if with the special design of showing that the sounds were not the responses of an echo—the steps sometimes slackened nearly to a halt, and sometimes hurried for six or eight strides to a run, and again abated to a walk. Captain Barton, as before, turned suddenly round, and with the same result—no object was visible above the deserted level of the road. He walked back over the same ground, determined that, whatever might have been the cause of the sounds which had so disconcerted him, it should not escape his search—the endeavour, however, was unrewarded. In spite of all his scepticism, he felt something like a superstitious fear stealing fast upon him, and with these unwonted and uncomfortable sensations, he once more turned and pursued his way. There was no repetition of these haunting sounds, until he had reached the point where he had last stopped to retrace his steps—here they were resumed—and with sudden starts of running, which threatened to bring the unseen pursuer close up to the alarmed pedestrian. Captain Barton arrested his course as formerly—the unaccountable nature of the occurrence filled him with vague and almost horrible sensations— and yielding to the excitement he felt gaining upon him, he shouted sternly, "Who goes there?" The sound of one's own voice, thus exerted, in utter solitude, and followed by total silence, has in it something unpleasantly exciting, and he felt a degree of nervousness which, perhaps, from no cause had he ever known before. To the very end of this solitary street the steps pursued him—and it required a strong effort of stubborn pride on his part to resist the impulse that prompted him every moment to run for safety at the top of his speed. It was not until he had reached his lodging, and sate by his own fire-side, that he felt sufficiently reassured to rearrange and reconsider in his own mind the occurrences which had so discomposed him. So little a matter, after all, is sufficient to upset the pride of scepticism and vindicate the old simple laws of nature within us.

Mr. Barton was next morning sitting at a late breakfast, reflecting upon the incidents of the previous night, with more of inquisitiveness than awe, so speedily do gloomy impressions upon the fancy disappear under the cheerful influences of day, when a letter just delivered by the postman was placed upon the table before him. There was nothing remarkable in the address of this missive, except that it was written in a hand which he did not know—perhaps it was disguised—for the tall narrow characters were sloped backward; and with the self-inflicted suspense which we so often see practised in such cases, he puzzled over the inscription for a full minute before he broke the seal. When he did so, he read the following words, written in the same hand:—

"Mr. Barton, late Captain of the 'Dolphin,' is warned of DANGER. He will do wisely to avoid —— street—[here the locality of his last night's adventure was named]—if he walks there as usual he will meet with something bad—let him take warning, once for all, for he has good reason to dread

"THE WATCHER."

Captain Barton read and re-read this strange effusion; in every light and in every direction he turned it over and over; he examined the paper on which it was written, and closely scrutinized the hand-writing even more. Defeated here, he turned to the seal; it was nothing but a patch of wax, upon which the accidental impression of a coarse thumb was imperfectly visible. There was not the slightest mark, no clue or indication of any kind, to lead him to even a guess as to its possible origin. The writer's object seemed a friendly one, and yet he subscribed himself as one whom he had "good reason to dread." Altogether the letter, its author, and its real purpose, were to him an inexplicable puzzle, and one, moreover, unpleasantly suggestive, in his mind, of associations connected with the last night's adventure.

In obedience to some feeling—perhaps of pride—Mr. Barton did not communicate, even to his intended bride, the occurrences which we have just detailed. Trifling as they might appear, they had in reality most disagreeably affected his imagination, and he cared not to disclose, even to the young lady in question, what she might possibly look upon as evidences of weakness. The letter might very well be but a hoax, and the mysterious footfall but a delusion of his fancy. But although he affected to treat the whole affair as unworthy of a thought, it yet haunted him pertinaciously, tormenting him with perplexing doubts, and depressing him with undefined apprehensions. Certain it is, that for a considerable time afterwards he carefully avoided the street indicated in the letter as the scene of danger.

It was not until about a week after the receipt of the letter which I have transcribed, that anything further occurred to remind Captain Barton of its contents, or to counteract the gradual disappearance from his mind of the disagreeable impressions which he had then received. He was returning one night, after the interval I have stated, from the theatre, which was then situated in Crow-street, and having there handed Miss Montague and Lady L——into their carriage, he loitered for some time with two or three acquaintances. With these, however, he parted close to the college, and pursued his way alone. It was now fully one o'clock, and the streets were quite deserted. During the whole of his walk with the companions from whom he had just parted, he had been at times painfully aware of the sound of steps, as it seemed, dogging them on their way. Once or twice he had looked back, in the uneasy anticipation that he was again about to experience the same mysterious annoyances which had so much disconcerted him a week before, and earnestly hoping that he might *see* some form from whom the sounds might naturally proceed. But the street was deserted—no form was visible. Proceeding now quite alone upon his homeward way, he grew really nervous and uncomfortable, as he became sensible, with increased distinctness, of the well-known and now absolutely dreaded sounds.

By the side of the dead wall which bounded the college park, the sounds followed, re-commencing almost simultaneously with his own steps. The same unequal pace—sometimes slow, sometimes for a score yards or so, quickened to a run—was audible from behind him. Again and again he turned; quickly and stealthily he glanced over his shoulder—almost at every half-dozen steps; but no one was visible. The horrors of this intangible and unseen persecution became gradually all but intolerable; and when at last he reached his home, his nerves were strung to such a pitch of excitement that he could not rest, and did not attempt even to lie down until after the day-light had broken.

He was awakened by a knock at his chamber-door, and his servant entering, handed him several letters which had just been received by the penny post. One among them instantly arrested his attention—a single glance at the direction aroused him thoroughly. He at once recognized its character, and read as follows:—

"You may as well think, Captain Barton, to escape from your own shadow as from me; do what you may, I will see you as often as I please, and you shall see me, for I do not want to hide myself, as you fancy. Do not let it trouble your rest, Captain

Barton; for, with a *good conscience*, what need you fear from the eye of

"THE WATCHER."

It is scarcely necessary to dwell upon the feelings elicited by a perusal of this strange communication. Captain Barton was observed to be unusually absent and out of spirits for several days afterwards; but no one divined the cause. Whatever he might think as to the phantom steps which followed him, there could be no possible illusion about the letters he had received; and, to say the least of it, their immediate sequence upon the mysterious sounds which had haunted him, was an odd coincidence. The whole circumstance was, in his own mind, vaguely and instinctively connected with certain passages in his past life, which, of all others, he hated to remember. It happened, however, that in addition to his own approaching nuptials, Captain Barton had just then—fortunately, perhaps, for himself—some business of an engrossing kind connected with the adjustment of a large and long-litigated claim upon certain properties. The hurry and excitement of business had its natural effect in gradually dispelling the marked gloom which had for a time occasionally oppressed him, and in a little while his spirits had entirely resumed their accustomed tone.

During all this time, however, he was occasionally dismayed by indistinct and half-heard repetitions of the same annoyance, and that in lonely places, in the day-time as well as after nightfall. These renewals of the strange impressions from which he had suffered so much were, however, desultory and faint, insomuch that often he really could not, to his own satisfaction, distinguish between them and the mere suggestions of an excited imagination.

One evening he walked down to the House of Commons with a member, an acquaintance of his and mine. This was one of the few occasions upon which I have been in company with Captain Barton. As we walked down together, I observed that he became absent and silent, and to a degree so marked as scarcely to consist with good breeding, and which, in one who was obviously, in all his habits, perfectly a gentleman, seemed to argue the pressure of some urgent and absorbing anxiety. I afterwards learned that, during the whole of our walk, he had heard the well-known footsteps dogging him as we proceeded. This, however, was the last time he suffered from this phase of the persecution, of which he was already the anxious victim. A new and a very different one was about to be presented.

Of the new series of impressions which were afterwards gradually to work out his destiny, I that evening witnessed the first; and but for its relation to the train of events which followed, the incident would scarcely have been now remembered by me. As we were walking in at the passage, a man, of whom I remember only that he was short in stature, looked like a foreigner, and wore a kind of travelling-cap, walked very rapidly, and as if under some fierce excitement, directly toward us, muttering to himself, fast and vehemently the while. This odd-looking person walked straight toward Barton, who was foremost of the three, and halted, regarding him for a moment or two with a look of menace and fury almost maniacal; and then turning about as abruptly, he walked before us at the same agitated pace, and disappeared at a side passage. I do distinctly remember being a good deal shocked at the countenance and bearing of this man, which indeed irresistibly impressed me with an undefined sense of danger, such as I have never felt before or since from the presence of anything human; but these sensations were, on my part, far from amounting to anything so disconcerting as to flurry or excite me—I had seen only a singularly evil countenance, agitated, as it seemed, with the excitement of madness. I was absolutely astonished, however, at the effect of this apparition upon Captain Barton. I knew him to be a man of proud courage and coolness in real danger—a circumstance which made his conduct upon this occasion the more conspicuously odd. He recoiled a step or two as the stranger advanced, and clutched my arm in silence, with what seemed to me to be a spasm of agony or terror; and then, as the figure disappeared, shoving me roughly back, he followed it for a few paces, stopped in great disorder, and sat down upon a form. I never beheld a countenance more ghastly and haggard.

"For God's sake, Barton, what is the matter?" said ———, our companion, really alarmed at his appearance. "You're not hurt, are you?—or unwell? What is it?"

"What did he say?—I did not hear it—what was it?" asked Barton, wholly disregarding the question.

"Tut, tut—nonsense," said ———, greatly surprised; "who cares what the fellow said. You are unwell, Barton—decidedly unwell; let me call a coach."

"Unwell! Yes—no—not exactly unwell," he said, evidently making an effort to recover his self-possession; "but, to say the truth, I am fatigued—a little over-worked—and perhaps over anxious. You know I have been in chancery, and the winding up of a suit is always a nervous affair. I have felt uncomfortable all this evening; but I am better now. Come, come; shall we go on?"

"No, no. Take my advice, Barton, and go home; you really do need rest; you are looking absolutely ill. I really do insist on your allowing me to see you home," replied his friend.

I seconded ———'s advice, the more readily as it was obvious that Barton was not himself disinclined to be persuaded. He left us, politely declining our offered escort. I was not sufficiently intimate with ——— to discuss the scene which we had both just witnessed, and in which his friend had appeared in so strange a light. I was, however, convinced, from his manner in the few common-place comments and regrets which we exchanged, that he was just was just as little satisfied as I with the extempore plea of illness with which he had accounted for the strange exhibition, and that we were both agreed in suspecting some lurking mystery in the matter.

I called next day at Barton's lodgings, to inquire for him, and learned from the servant that he had not left his room since his return the night before; but that he was not seriously indisposed, and hoped to be out again in a few days. That evening he sent for Doctor R———, then in large and fashionable practice in Dublin, and their interview was, it is said, an odd one.

He entered into a detail of his own symptoms in an abstracted and desultory kind of way, which seemed to argue a strange want of interest in his own cure, and, at all events, made it manifest that there was some topic engaging his mind of more engrossing importance than his present ailment. He complained of occasional palpitations and headache. Doctor R——— asked him, among other questions, whether there was any irritating circumstance or anxiety then occupying his thoughts. This he denied quickly and almost peevishly; and the physician thereupon declared his opinion, that there was nothing amiss except some slight derangement of the digestion, for which he accordingly wrote a prescription, and was about to withdraw, when Mr. Barton, with the air of a man who suddenly recollects a topic which had nearly escaped him, recalled him.

"I beg your pardon, doctor, but I had really almost forgot; will you permit me to ask you two or three medical questions—rather odd ones, perhaps, but as a wager depends upon their solution, you will, I hope, excuse my unreasonableness."

The physician readily undertook to satisfy the inquirer.

Barton seemed to have some difficulty about opening the proposed interrogatories, for he was silent for a minute, then walked to his book-case, and returned as he had gone; at last he sat down, and said—

"You'll think them very childish questions, but I can't recover my wager without a decision; so I must put them. I want to know first about lock-jaw. If a man actually has had that complaint, and appears to have died of it—so much so, that a physician of average skill pronounces him actually dead—may he, after all, recover?"

The physician smiled, and shook his head.

"But—but a blunder may be made," resumed Barton. "Suppose an ignorant pretender to medical skill; may *he* be so deceived by any stage of the complaint, as to mistake what is only a part of the progress of the disease, for death itself?"

"No one who had ever seen death," answered he, "could mistake it in a case of lock-jaw."

Barton mused for a few minutes. "I am going to ask you a question, perhaps, still more childish; but first, tell me, are not the regulations of foreign hospitals, such as that of, let us say, ———, very lax and bungling. May not all kinds of blunders and slips occur in their entries of names, and so forth?"

Doctor R—— professed his incompetence to answer that query.

"Well, then, doctor, here is the last of my questions. You will, probably, laugh at it; but it must out, nevertheless.

Is there any disease, in all the range of human maladies, which would have the effect of perceptibly contracting the stature, and the whole frame—causing the man to shrink in all his proportions, and yet to preserve his exact resemblance to himself in every particular—with the one exception, his height and bulk; *any* disease, mark—no matter how rare—how little believed in, generally—which could possibly result in producing such an effect?"

The physician replied with a smile, and a very decided negative.

"Tell me, then," said Barton, abruptly, "if a man be in reasonable fear of assault from a lunatic who is at large, can he not procure a warrant for his arrest and detention?"

"Really, that is more a lawyer's question than one in my way," replied Doctor R——; "but I believe, on applying to a magistrate, such a course would be directed."

The physician then took his leave; but, just as he reached the hall-door, remembered that he had left his cane up stairs, and returned. His reappearance was awkward, for a piece of paper, which he recognized as his own prescription, was slowly burning upon the fire, and Barton sitting close by with an expression of settled gloom and dismay. Doctor R—— had too much tact to appear to observe what presented itself; but he had seen quite enough to assure him that the mind, and not the body, of Captain Barton was in reality the seat of his suffering.

A few days afterwards, the following advertisement appeared in the Dublin newspapers:—

"If Sylvester Yelland, formerly a foremast-man on board his Majesty's frigate Dolphin, or his nearest of kin, will apply to Mr. Robert Smith, solicitor, at his office, Dame-street, he or they may hear of something greatly to his or their advantage. Admission may be had at any hour up to twelve o'clock at night, for the next fortnight, should parties desire to avoid observation; and the strictest secrecy, as to all communications intended to be confidential, shall be honourably observed."

The Dolphin, as I have mentioned, was the vessel which Captain Barton had commanded; and this circumstance, connected with the extraordinary exertions made by the circulation of hand-bills, &c., as well as by repeated advertisements, to secure for this strange notice the utmost possible publicity, suggested to Doctor R—— the idea that Captain Barton's extreme uneasiness was somehow connected with the individual to whom the advertisement was addressed, and he himself the author of it. This, however, it is needless to add, was no more than a conjecture. No information whatsoever, as to the real purpose of the advertisement itself, was divulged by the agent, nor yet any hint as to who his employer might be.

Mr. Barton, although he had latterly begun to earn for himself the character of a hypochondriac, was yet very far from deserving it. Though by no means lively, he had yet, naturally, what are termed "even spirits," and was not subject to undue depressions. He soon, therefore, began to return to his former habits; and one of the earliest symptoms of this healthier tone of spirits was, his appearing at a grand dinner of the Freemasons, of which worthy fraternity he was himself a brother. Barton, who had been at first gloomy and abstracted, drank much more freely than was his wont—possibly with the purpose of dispelling his own secret anxieties—and under the influence of good wine, and pleasant company, became gradually (unlike his usual *self*) talkative, and even noisy. It was under this unwonted excitement that he left his company at about half-past ten o'clock; and, as conviviality is a strong incentive to gallantry, it occurred to him to proceed forthwith to Lady L——'s, and pass the remainder of the evening with her and his destined bride.

Accordingly, he was soon at —— street, and chatting gaily with the ladies. It is not to be supposed that Capt. Barton had exceeded the limits which propriety prescribes to good fellowship—he had merely taken enough of wine to raise his spirits, without, however, in the least degree unsteadying his mind, or affecting his manners. With this undue elevation of spirits had supervened an entire oblivion or contempt of those undefined apprehensions which had for so long weighed upon his mind, and to a certain extent estranged him from society; but as the night wore away, and his artificial gaiety began to flag, these painful feelings gradually intruded themselves again, and he grew abstracted and anxious as heretofore. He took his leave at length, with an unpleasant foreboding of some coming mischief, and with a mind haunted with a thousand mysterious apprehensions, such as, even while he acutely felt their pressure, he, nevertheless, inwardly strove, or affected to contemn.

It was this proud defiance of what he considered as his own weakness, which prompted him upon the present occasion to that course which brought about the adventure which we are now about to relate. Mr. Barton might have easily called a coach, but he was conscious that his strong inclination to do so proceeded from no cause other than what he desperately persisted in representing to himself to be his own superstitious tremors. He might also have returned home by a *route* different from that against which he had been warned by his mysterious correspondent; but for the same reason he dismissed this idea also, and with a dogged and half desperate resolution to force matters to a crisis of some kind, if there were any reality in the causes of his former suffering, and if not, satisfactorily to bring their delusiveness to the proof, he determined to follow precisely the course which he had trodden upon the night so painfully memorable in his own mind as that on which his strange persecution had commenced. Though, sooth to say, the pilot who for the first time steers his vessel under the muzzles of a hostile battery, never felt his resolution more severely tasked than did Captain Barton as he breathlessly pursued this solitary path—a path which, spite of every effort of scepticism and reason, he felt to be infested by some (as respected *him*) malignant influence.

He pursued his way steadily and rapidly, scarcely breathing from intensity of suspense; he, however, was troubled by no renewal of the dreaded footsteps, and was beginning to feel a return of confidence, as, more than three-fourths of the way being accomplished with impunity, he approached the long line of twinkling oil lamps which indicated the frequented streets. This feeling of self-gratulation was, however, but momentary. The report of a musket at some two hundred yards behind him, and the whistle of a bullet close to his head, disagreeably and startlingly dispelled it. His first impulse was to retrace his steps in pursuit of the assassin; but the road on either side was, as we have said, embarrassed by the foundations of a street, beyond which extended waste fields, full of rubbish and neglected lime and brick kilns, and all now as utterly silent as though no sound had ever disturbed their dark and unsightly solitude. The futility of, single-handed, attempting, under such circumstances, a search for the murderer, was apparent, especially as no sound, either of retreating steps or otherwise, was audible to direct his pursuit.

With the tumultuous sensations of one whose life has just been exposed to a murderous attempt, and whose escape has been the narrowest possible, Captain Barton turned, and without, however, quickening his pace actually to a run, hurriedly pursued his way. He had turned, as we have said, after a pause of a few seconds, and had just commenced his rapid retreat, when on a sudden he met the well-remembered little man in the fur cap. The encounter was but momentary. The figure was walking at the same exaggerated pace, and with the same strange air of menace as before; and as it passed him, he thought he heard it say, in a furious whisper, "Still alive—still alive!"

The state of Mr. Barton's spirits began now to work a corresponding alteration in his health and looks, and to such a degree that it was impossible that the change should escape general remark. For some reasons, known but to himself, he took no step whatsoever to bring the attempt upon his life, which he had so narrowly escaped, under the notice of the authorities; on the contrary, he kept it jealously to himself; and it was not for many weeks after the occurrence that he mentioned it, and then in strict confidence, to a gentleman, whom the torments of his mind at last compelled him to consult.

Spite of his blue devils, however, poor Barton, having no satisfactory reason to render to the public for any undue remissness in the attentions which the relation subsisting between him and Miss Montague required, was obliged to exert himself, and present to the world a confident and cheerful bearing. The true source of his sufferings, and every circumstance connected with them, he guarded with a reserve so jealous, that it seemed dictated by at least a suspicion that the origin of his strange persecution was known to himself, and that it was of a nature which, upon his own account, he could not or dared not disclose.

The mind thus turned in upon itself, and constantly occupied with a haunting anxiety which it dared not reveal, or confide to any human breast, became daily more excited, and, of course, more vividly impressible, by a system of attack which operated through the nervous system; and in this state he was destined to sustain, with increasing frequency, the stealthy visitations of that apparition which from the first had seemed to possess so unearthly and terrible a hold upon his imagination.

ℇ

It was about this time that Captain Barton called upon the then celebrated preacher, Dr. ———, with whom he had a slight acquaintance, and an extraordinary conversation ensued. The divine was seated in his chambers in college, surrounded with works upon his favourite pursuit, and deep in theology, when Barton was announced. There was something at once embarrassed and excited in his manner, which, along with his wan and haggard countenance, impressed the student with the unpleasant consciousness that his visitor must have recently suffered terribly indeed, to account for an alteration so striking—almost shocking.

After the usual interchange of polite greeting, and a few common-place remarks, Captain Barton, who obviously perceived the surprise which his visit had excited, and which Doctor ——— was unable wholly to conceal, interrupted a brief pause by remarking—

"This is a strange call, Doctor ———, perhaps scarcely warranted by an acquaintance so slight as mine with you. I should not, under ordinary circumstances have ventured to disturb you; but my visit is neither an idle nor impertinent intrusion. I am sure you will not so account it, when—"

Doctor ——— interrupted him with assurances such as good breeding suggested, and Barton resumed—

"I am come to task your patience by asking your advice. When I say your patience, I might, indeed, say more; I might have said your humanity—your compassion; for I have been, and am a great sufferer."

"My dear sir," replied the churchman, "it will, indeed, afford me infinite gratification if I can give you comfort in any distress of mind; but—but—"

"I know what you would say," resumed Barton, quickly; "I am an unbeliever, and, therefore, incapable of deriving help from religion; but don't take that for granted. At least you must not assume that, however unsettled my convictions may be, I do not feel a deep—a very deep—interest in the subject. Circumstances have lately forced it upon my attention, in such a way as to compel me to review the whole question in a more candid and teachable spirit, I believe, than I ever studied it in before."

"Your difficulties, I take it for granted, refer to the evidences of revelation," suggested the clergyman.

"Why—no—yes; in fact I am ashamed to say I have not considered even my objections sufficiently to state them connectedly; but—but there is one subject on which I feel a peculiar interest."

He paused again, and Doctor —— pressed him to proceed.

"The fact is," said Barton, "whatever may be my uncertainty as to the authenticity of what we are taught to call revelation, of one fact I am deeply and horribly convinced, that there does exist beyond this a spiritual world—a system whose workings are generally in mercy hidden from us—a system which may be, and which is sometimes, partially and terribly revealed. I am sure—I *know*," continued Barton, with increasing excitement, "there is a God—a dreadful God—and that retribution follows guilt. In ways the most mysterious and stupendous—by agencies, the most inexplicable and terrific—

there is a spiritual system—great God, how frightfully I have been convinced!—a system malignant, and implacable, and omnipotent, under whose persecutions I am, and have been, suffering the torments of the damned!—yes, sir—yes—the fires and frenzy of hell!"

As Barton spoke, his agitation became so vehement that the divine was shocked, and even alarmed. The wild and excited rapidity with which he spoke, and, above all, the indefinable horror which stamped his features, afforded a contrast to his ordinary cool and unimpassioned self-possession striking and painful in the last degree.

"My dear sir," said Doctor ——, after a brief pause, "I fear you have been suffering much, indeed; but I venture to predict that the depression under which you labour will be found to originate in purely physical causes, and that with a change of air, and the aid of a few tonics, your spirits will return, and the tone of your mind be once more cheerful and tranquil as heretofore. There was, after all, more truth than we are quite willing to admit in the classic theories which assigned the undue predominance of any one affection of the mind, to the undue action or torpidity of one or other of our bodily organs. Believe me, that a little attention to diet, exercise, and the other essentials of health, under competent direction, will make you as much yourself as you can wish."

"Doctor ——," said Barton, with something like a shudder, "I *cannot* delude myself with such a hope. I have no hope to cling to but one, and that is, that by some other spiritual agency more potent than that which tortures me, *it* may be combated, and I delivered. If this may not be, I am lost—now and for ever lost."

"But, Mr. Barton, you must remember," urged his companion, "that others have suffered as you have done, and—"

"No, no, no," interrupted he, with irritability; "no, sir, I am not a credulous—far from a superstitious man. I have been, perhaps, too much the reverse—too sceptical, too slow of belief; but unless I were one whom no amount of evidence could convince, unless I were to contemn the repeated, the *perpetual* evidence of my own senses, I am now—now at last constrained to believe—I have no escape from the conviction—the overwhelming certainty—that I am haunted and dogged, go where I may, by—by a DEMON."

There was an almost preternatural energy of horror in Barton's face, as, with its damp and deathlike lineaments turned towards his companion, he thus delivered himself.

"God help you, my poor friend," said Doctor ——, much shocked—, "God help you; for, indeed, you *are* a sufferer, however your sufferings may have been caused."

"Ay, ay, God help me," echoed Barton sternly; "but *will* he help me—will he help me?"

"Pray to him—pray in an humble and trusting spirit," said he.

"Pray, pray," echoed he again; "I can't pray—I could as easily move a mountain by an effort of my will. I have not belief enough to pray; there is something within me that will not pray. You prescribe impossibilities—literal impossibilities."

"You will not find it so, if you will but try," said Doctor ——.

"Try!—I *have* tried, and the attempt only fills me with confusion and terror; I have tried in vain, and more than in vain. The awful, unutterable idea of eternity and infinity oppresses and maddens my brain, whenever my mind approaches the contemplation of the Creator; I recoil from the effort, scared, confounded, terrified. I tell you, Doctor ——, if I am to be saved, it must be by other means. The idea of the Creator is to me intolerable—my mind cannot support it."

"Say, then, my dear sir," urged he—"say how you would have me serve you—what you would learn of me—what can I do or say to relieve you?"

"Listen to me first," replied Captain Barton, with a subdued air, and an evident effort to suppress his excitement—"listen to me while I detail the circumstances of the terrible persecution under which my life has become all but intolerable—a persecution which has made me fear *death* and the world beyond the grave as much as I have grown to hate existence."

Barton then proceeded to relate the circumstances which we have already detailed, and then continued—

"This has now become habitual—an accustomed thing. I do not mean the actual seeing him in the flesh—thank God, *that* at least is not permitted daily. Thank God, from the unutterable horrors of that visitation I have been mercifully allowed intervals of repose, though none of security; but from the consciousness that a malignant spirit is following and watching me wherever I go, I have never, for a single instant, a temporary respite. I am pursued with blasphemies, cries of despair and appalling hatred. I hear those dreadful sounds called after me as I turn the corners of streets; they come in the night-time, while I sit in my chamber alone; they haunt me everywhere, charging me with hideous crimes, and—great God!—threatening me with coming vengeance and eternal misery. Hush!—do you hear *that!*" he cried with a horrible smile of triumph; "there—there, will that convince you?"

The clergyman felt the chillness of horror irresistibly steal over him, while, during the wail of a sudden gust of wind, he heard, or fancied he heard, the half articulate sounds of rage and derision mingling in the sough.

"Well, what do you think of *that?*" at length Barton cried, drawing a long breath through his teeth.

"I heard the wind," said Doctor ———. "What should I think of it—what is there remarkable about it?"

"The prince of the powers of the air," muttered Barton, with a shudder.

"Tut, tut! my dear sir," said the student, with an effort to reassure himself; for though it was broad daylight, there was nevertheless something disagreeably contagious in the nervous excitement under which his visitor so obviously suffered. "You must not give way to those wild fancies; you must resist these impulses of the imagination."

"Ay, ay; 'resist the devil and he will flee from thee'," said Barton in the same tone; "but *how* resist him? ay, there it is—there is the rub. What—*what* am I to do? what *can* I do?"

"My dear sir, this is fancy," said the man of folios; "you are your own tormentor."

"No, no, sir—fancy has no part in it," answered Barton, somewhat sternly. "Fancy, forsooth! Was it that made *you*, as well as me, hear, but this moment, those appalling accents of hell? Fancy, indeed! No, no."

"But you have seen this person frequently," said the ecclesiastic;—"why have you not accosted or secured him? Is it not somewhat precipitate, to say no more, to assume, as you have done, the existence of preternatural agency, when, after all, everything may be easily accountable, if only proper means were taken to sift the matter."

"There are circumstances connected with this—this *appearance*," said Barton, "which it were needless to disclose, but which to *me* are proofs of its horrible and unearthly nature. I know that the being who haunts me is not *man*—I say I *know* this; I could prove it to your own conviction." He paused for a minute, and then added, "And as to accosting it, I dare not, I could not; when I see it I am powerless; I stand in the gaze of death, in the triumphant presence of preter-human power and malignity. My strength, and faculties, and memory all forsake me. O God, I fear, sir, you know not what you speak of. Mercy, mercy; heaven have pity on me!"

He leaned his elbow on the table, and passed his hand across his eyes, as if to exclude some image of horror, muttering the last words of the sentence he had just concluded, again and again.

"Doctor ——," he said, abruptly raising himself, and looking full upon the clergyman with an imploring eye, "I know you will do for me whatever may be done. You know now fully the circumstances and the nature of the mysterious agency of which I am the victim. I tell you I cannot help myself; I cannot hope to escape; I am utterly passive. I conjure you, then, to weigh my case well, and if anything may be done for me by vicarious supplication—by the intercession of the good—or by any aid or influence whatsoever, I implore of you, I adjure you in the name of the Most High, give me the benefit of that influence—deliver me from the body of this death. Strive for me, pity me; I know you will; you cannot refuse this; it is the purpose and object of my visit. Send me away with some hope, however little, some faint hope of ultimate deliverance, and I will nerve myself to endure, from hour to hour, the hideous dream into which my existence has been transformed."

Doctor —— assured him that all he could do was to pray earnestly for him, and that so much he would not fail to do. They parted with a hurried and melancholy valediction. Barton hastened to the carriage, which awaited him at the door, drew the blinds, and drove away, while Dr. —— returned to his chamber, to ruminate at leisure upon the strange interview which had just interrupted his studies.

It was not to be expected that Captain Barton's changed and eccentric habits should long escape remark and discussion. Various were the theories suggested to account for it. Some attributed the alteration to the pressure of secret pecuniary embarrassments; others to a repugnance to fulfil an engagement into which he was presumed to have too precipitately entered; and others, again, to the supposed incipiency of mental disease, which latter, indeed, was the most plausible, as well as the most generally received, of the hypotheses circulated in the gossip of the day.

From the very commencement of this change, at first so gradual in its advances, Miss Montague had of course been aware of it. The intimacy involved in their peculiar relation, as well as the near interest which it inspired, afforded, in her case, a like opportunity and motive for the successful exercise of that keen and penetrating observation peculiar to the sex. His visits became, at length, so interrupted, and his manner, while they lasted, so abstracted, strange, and agitated, that Lady L——, after hinting her anxiety and her suspicions more than once, at length distinctly stated her anxiety, and pressed for an explanation. The explanation was given, and although its nature at first relieved the worse solicitudes of the old lady and her niece, yet the circumstances which attended it, and the really dreadful consequences which it obviously indicated as regarded the spirits, and indeed the reason of the now wretched man, who made the strange declaration, were enough, upon a little reflection, to fill their minds with perturbation and alarm.

General Montague, the young lady's father, at length arrived. He had himself slightly known Barton, some ten or twelve years previously, and being aware of his fortune and connexions, was disposed to regard him as an unexceptionable and indeed a most desirable match for his daughter. He laughed at the story of Barton's supernatural visitations, and lost not a moment in calling upon his intended son-in-law.

"My dear Barton," he continued, gaily, after a little conversation, "my sister tells me that you are a victim to blue devils, in quite a new and original shape."

Barton changed countenance, and sighed profoundly.

"Come, come; I protest this will never do," continued the general; "you are more like a man on his way to the gallows than to the altar. These devils have made quite a saint of you."

Barton made an effort to change the conversation.

"No, no, it won't do," said his visitor laughing; "I am resolved to say out what I have to say upon this magnificent mock mystery of yours. Come, you must not be angry, but really it is too bad to see you, at your time of life, absolutely frightened into good behaviour, like a naughty child, by a bugaboo, and, as far as I can learn, a very particularly contemptible one. Seriously, though, my dear Barton, I have been a good deal annoyed at what they tell me; but, at the same time, thoroughly convinced that there is nothing in the matter that may not be cleared up, with just a little attention and management, within a week at furthest."

"Ah, general, you do not know——" he began.

"Yes, but I do know quite enough to warrant my confidence," interrupted the soldier; "don't I know that all your annoyance proceeds from the occasional appearance of a certain little man in a cap and great-coat, with a red vest and a bad face, who follows you about, and pops upon you at the corners of lanes, and throws you into ague fits. Now, my dear fellow, I'll make it my business to *catch* this mischievous little mountebank, and either beat him into a jelly with my own hands, or have him whipped through the town at the cart's-tail, before a month passes."

"If *you* knew what *I* know," said Barton, with gloomy agitation, "you would speak very differently. Don't imagine that I am so weak and foolish as to assume, without proof the most overwhelming, the conclusion to which I have been forced—the proofs are here, locked up here." As he spoke he tapped upon his breast, and with an anxious sigh continued to walk up and down the room.

"Well, well, Barton," said his visitor, "I'll wager a rump and dozen I collar the ghost, and convince yourself before many days are over."

He was running on in the same strain when he was suddenly arrested, and not a little shocked, by observing Barton, who had approached the window, stagger slowly back, like one who had received a stunning blow; his arm feebly extended toward the street—his face and his very lips white as ashes—while he muttered, "There—there—there!"

General Montague started mechanically to his feet, and, from the window of the drawing-room, saw a figure corresponding, as well as his hurry would permit him to discern, with the description of the person, whose appearance so constantly and dreadfully disturbed the repose of his friend. The figure was just turning from the rails of the area upon which it had been leaning, and, without waiting to see more, the old gentleman snatched his cane and hat, and rushed down the stairs and into the street, in the furious hope of securing the person, and punishing the audacity of the mysterious stranger. He looked around him, but in vain, for any trace of the form he had himself distinctly beheld. He ran breathlessly to the nearest corner, expecting to see from thence the retreating figure, but no such form was visible. Back and forward, from crossing to crossing, he ran, at fault, and it was not until the curious gaze and laughing countenances of the passers-by reminded him of the absurdity of his pursuit, that he checked his hurried pace, lowered his walking-cane from the menacing altitude which he had mechanically given it, adjusted his hat, and walked composedly back again, inwardly vexed and flurried. He found Barton pale and trembling in every joint; they both remained silent, though under emotions very different. At last Barton whispered, "You saw it?"

"*It!*—him—some one—you mean—to be sure I did," replied Montague, testily. "But where is the good or the harm of seeing him? The fellow runs like a lamp-lighter. I wanted to *catch* him, but he had stolen away before I could reach the hall-door. However, it is no great matter; next time, I dare say, I'll do better; and, egad, if I once come within reach of him, I'll introduce his shoulders to the weight of my cane, in a way to make him cry *peccavi*."

Notwithstanding General Montague's undertakings and exhortations, however, Barton continued to suffer from the self-same unexplained cause; go how, when, or where he would, he was still constantly dogged or confronted by the hateful being who had established over him so dreadful and mysterious an influence; nowhere and at no time was he secure against the odious appearance which haunted him with such diabolic perseverance. His depression, misery, and excitement became more settled and alarming every day, and the mental agonies that ceaselessly preyed upon him, began at last so sensibly to affect his general health, that Lady L—— and General Montague succeeded, without, indeed, much difficulty, in persuading him to try a short tour on the Continent, in the hope that an entire change of scene would, at all events, have the effect of breaking through the influences of local association, which the more sceptical of his friends assumed to be by no means inoperative in suggesting and perpetuating what they conceived to be a mere form of nervous illusion. General Montague indeed was persuaded that the figure which haunted his intended son-in-law was by no means the creation of his own imagination, but, on the contrary, a substantial form of flesh and blood, animated by a spiteful and obstinate resolution, perhaps with some murderous object in perspective, to watch and follow the unfortunate gentleman. Even this hypothesis was not a very pleasant one; yet it was plain that if Barton could ever be convinced that there was nothing preternatural in the phenomenon which he had hitherto regarded in that light, the affair would lose all its terrors in his eyes, and wholly cease to exercise upon his health and spirits the baleful influence which it had hitherto done. He therefore reasoned, that if the annoyance were actually escaped from by mere locomotion and change of scene, it obviously could not have originated in any supernatural agency.

Yielding to their persuasions, Barton left Dublin for England, accompanied by General Montague. They posted rapidly to London, and thence to Dover, whence they took the packet with a fair wind for Calais. The general's confidence in the result of the expedition on Barton's spirits had risen day by day since their departure from the shores of Ireland; for, to the inexpressible relief and delight of the latter, he had not, since then, so much as even once fancied a repetition of those impressions which had, when at home, drawn him gradually down to the very depths of horror and despair. This exemption from what he had begun to regard as the inevitable condition of his existence, and the sense of security which began to pervade his mind, were inexpressibly delightful; and in the exultation of what he considered his deliverance, he indulged in a thousand happy anticipations for a future into which so lately he had hardly dared to look; and in short, both he and his companion secretly congratulated themselves upon the termination of that persecution which had been to its immediate victim a source of such unspeakable agony.

It was a beautiful day, and a crowd of idlers stood upon the jetty to receive the packet, and enjoy the bustle of the new arrivals. Montague walked a few paces in advance of his friend, and as he made his way through the crowd, a little man touched his arm, and said to him, in a broad provincial *patois*—

"Monsieur is walking too fast; he will lose his sick comrade in the throng, for, by my faith, the poor gentleman seems to be fainting."

Montague turned quickly, and observed that Barton did indeed look deadly pale. He hastened to his side.

"My dear fellow, are you ill?" he asked anxiously.

The question was unheeded and twice repeated, ere Barton stammered—

"I saw him—by ——, I saw him!"

"*Him!*—the—the wretch—who—where—when did you see him—where is he?" cried Montague, looking around him.

"I saw him—but he is gone," repeated Barton, faintly.

"But where—where? For God's sake, speak," urged Montague, vehemently.

"It is but this moment—*here*," said he.

"But what did he look like—what had he on—what did he wear—quick, quick," urged his excited companion, ready to dart among the crowd, and collar the delinquent on the spot.

"He touched your arm—he spoke to you—he pointed to me. God be merciful to me, there is no escape," said Barton, in the low, subdued tones of intense despair.

Montague had already bustled away in all the flurry of mingled hope and indignation; but though the singular *personnel* of the stranger who had accosted him was vividly and perfectly impressed upon his recollection, he failed to discover among the crowd even the slightest resemblance to him. After a fruitless search, in which he enlisted the services of several of the bystanders, who aided all the more zealously, as they believed he had been robbed, he at length, out of breath and baffled, gave over the attempt.

"Ah, my friend, it won't do," said Barton, with the faint voice and bewildered, ghastly look of one who has been stunned by some mortal shock; "there is no use in contending with it; whatever it is, the dreadful association between me and it is now established—I shall never escape—never, never!"

"Nonsense, nonsense, my dear fellow; don't talk so," said Montague, with something at once of irritation and dismay; "you must not, I say; we'll jockey the scoundrel yet; never mind, I say—never mind."

It was, however, but lost labour to endeavour henceforward to inspire Barton with one ray of hope; he became utterly desponding. This intangible, and as it seemed, utterly inadequate influence was fast destroying his energies of intellect, character, and health. His first object was now to return to Ireland, there, as he believed, and now almost hoped, speedily to die.

To Ireland, accordingly, he came, and one of the first faces he saw upon the shore was again that of his implacable and dreaded persecutor. Barton seemed at last to have lost not only all enjoyment and every hope in existence, but all independence of will besides. He now submitted himself passively to the management of the friends most nearly interested in his welfare. With the apathy of entire despair, he implicitly assented to whatever measures they suggested and advised; and as a last resource, it was determined to remove him to a house of Lady L——'s in the neighbourhood of Clontarf, where, with the advice of his medical attendant, who persisted in his opinion that the whole train of consequences resulted merely from some nervous derangement, it was resolved that he was to confine himself strictly to the house, and to make use only of those apartments which commanded a view of an enclosed yard, the gates of which were to be kept jealously locked. Those precautions would certainly secure him against the casual appearance of any living form, which his excited imagination might possibly confound with the spectre which, as it was contended, his fancy recognised in every figure which bore even a distant or general resemblance to the traits with which he had at first invested it. A month or six weeks' absolute seclusion under these conditions, it was hoped might, by interrupting the series of these terrible impressions, gradually dispel the predisposing apprehensions, and effectually break up the associations which had confirmed the supposed disease, and rendered recovery hopeless. Cheerful society and that of his friends was to be constantly supplied, and on the whole, very sanguine expectations were indulged in, that under the treatment thus detailed, the obstinate hypochondria of the patient might at length give way.

Accompanied, therefore, by Lady L——, General Montague, and his daughter—his own affianced bride—poor Barton—himself never daring to cherish a hope of his ultimate emancipation from the strange horrors under which his life was literally wasting away—took possession of the apartments, whose situation protected him against the dreadful intrusions, from which he shrunk with such unutterable terror.

After a little time, a steady persistence in this system began to manifest its results, in a very marked though gradual improvement, alike in the health and spirits of the invalid. Not, indeed, that anything at all approaching complete recovery was yet discernible. On the contrary, to those who had not seen him since the commencement of his strange sufferings, such an alteration would have been apparent as might well have shocked them. The improvement, however, such as it was, was welcomed with gratitude and delight, especially by the poor young lady, whom her attachment to him, as well as her now singularly painful position, consequent on his mysterious and protracted illness, rendered an object of pity scarcely one degree less to be commiserated than himself.

A week passed—a fortnight—a month—and yet no recurrence of the hated visitation had agitated and terrified him as usual. The treatment had, so far forth, been followed by complete success. The chain of association had been broken. The constant pressure upon the overtasked spirits had been removed, and, under these comparatively favourable circumstances, the sense of social community with the world about him, and something of human interest, if not of enjoyment, began to reanimate his mind.

It was about this time that Lady L———, who, like most old ladies of the day, was deep in family receipts, and a great pretender to medical science, being engaged in the concoction of certain unpalatable mixtures, of marvellous virtue, dispatched her own maid to the kitchen garden, with a list of herbs, which were there to be carefully culled, and brought back to her for the purpose stated. The handmaiden, however, returned with her task scarce half completed, and a good deal flurried and alarmed. Her mode of accounting for her precipitate retreat and evident agitation was odd, and to the old lady, unpleasantly startling.

It appeared that she had repaired to the kitchen garden, pursuant to her mistress's directions, and had there begun to make the specified selection among the rank and neglected herbs which crowded one corner of the enclosure, and while engaged in this pleasant labour, she carelessly sang a fragment of an old song, as she said, "to keep herself company." She was, however, interrupted by an ill-natured laugh; and, looking up, she saw through the old thorn hedge, which surrounded the garden, a singularly ill-looking little man, whose countenance wore the stamp of menace and malignity, standing close to her, at the other side of the hawthorn screen. She described herself as utterly unable to move or speak, while he charged her with a message for Captain Barton; the substance of which she distinctly remembered to have been to the effect, that he, Captain Barton, must come abroad as usual, and show himself to his friends, out of doors, or else prepare for a visit in his own chamber. On concluding this brief message, the stranger had, with a threatening air, got down into the outer ditch, and seizing the hawthorn stems in his hands, seemed on the point of climbing through the fence—a feat which might have been accomplished without much difficulty. Without, of course, awaiting this result, the girl—throwing down her treasures of thyme and rosemary—had turned and run, with the swiftness of terror, to the house. Lady L—— commanded her, on pain of instant dismissal, to observe an absolute silence respecting all that portion of the incident which related to Captain Barton; and, at the same time, directed instant search to be made, by her men in the garden and fields adjacent. This measure, however, was attended with the usual unsuccess, and, filled with fearful and undefinable misgivings, Lady L—— communicated the incident to her brother. The story, however, until long afterwards, went no further, and, of course, it was jealously guarded from Barton, who continued to amend, though slowly and imperfectly.

Barton now began to walk occasionally in the court-yard which we have mentioned, and which being surrounded by a high wall, commanded no view beyond its own extent. Here he, therefore, considered himself perfectly secure; and, but for a careless violation of orders by one of the grooms, he might have enjoyed, at least for some time longer, his much-prized immunity. Opening upon the public road, this yard was entered by a wooden gate, with a wicket in it, which was further defended by an iron gate upon the outside. Strict orders had been given to keep them carefully locked; but, spite of these, it had happened that one day, as Barton was slowly pacing this narrow enclosure, in his accustomed walk, and reaching the further extremity, was turning to retrace his steps, he saw the boarded wicket ajar, and the face of his tormentor immovably looking at him through the iron bars. For a few seconds he stood riveted to the earth—breathless and bloodless—in the fascination of that dreaded gaze, and then fell helplessly and insensibly upon the pavement.

There he was found a few minutes afterwards, and conveyed to his room—the apartment which he was never afterwards to leave alive. Henceforward a marked and unaccountable change was observable in the tone of his mind. Captain Barton was now no longer the excited and despairing man he had been before; a strange alteration had passed upon him—an unearthly tranquillity reigned in his mind—it was the anticipated stillness of the grave.

"Montague, my friend, this struggle is nearly ended now," he said, tranquilly, but with a look of fixed and fearful awe. "I have, at last, some comfort from that world of spirits, from which my punishment has come. I know now that my sufferings will soon be over."

Montague pressed him to speak on.

"Yes," said he, in a softened voice, "my punishment is nearly ended. From sorrow, perhaps, I shall never, in time or eternity, escape; but my *agony* is almost over. Comfort has been revealed to me, and what remains of my allotted struggle I will bear with submission—even with hope."

"I am glad to hear you speak so tranquilly, my dear fellow," said Montague; "peace and cheer of mind are all you need to make you what you were."

"No, no—I never can be that," said he, mournfully. "I am no longer fit for life. I am soon to die: I do not shrink from death as I did. I am to see *him* but once again, and then all is ended."

"He said so, then?" suggested Montague.

"*He?*—No, no: good tidings could scarcely come through him; and these were good and welcome; and they came so solemnly and sweetly—with unutterable love and melancholy, such as I could not—without saying more than is needful, or fitting, of other long-past scenes and persons—fully explain to you." As Barton said this he shed tears.

"Come, come," said Montague, mistaking the source of his emotions, "you must not give way. What is it, after all, but a pack of dreams and nonsense; or, at worst, the practices of a scheming rascal that enjoys his power of playing upon your nerves, and loves to exert it—a sneaking vagabond that owes you a grudge, and pays it off this way, not daring to try a more manly one."

"A grudge, indeed, he owes me—you say rightly," said Barton, with a sullen shudder; "a grudge, as you call it. Oh, my God! when the justice of heaven permits the Evil one to carry out a scheme of vengeance—when its execution is committed to the lost and terrible victim of sin, who owes his own ruin to the man, the very man, whom he is commissioned to pursue—then, indeed, the torments and terrors of hell are anticipated on earth. But heaven has dealt mercifully with me—hope has opened to me at last; and if death could come without the dreadful sight I am doomed to see, I would gladly close my eyes this moment upon the world. But though death is welcome, I shrink with an agony you cannot understand—a maddening agony, an actual frenzy of terror—from the last encounter with that—that DEMON, who has drawn me thus to the verge of the chasm, and who is himself to plunge me down. I am to see him again—once more—but under circumstances unutterably more terrific than ever."

As Barton thus spoke, he trembled so violently that Montague was really alarmed at the extremity of his sudden agitation, and hastened to lead him back to the topic which had before seemed to exert so tranquillizing an effect upon his mind.

"It was not a dream," he said, after a time; "I was in a different state—I felt differently and strangely; and yet it was all as real, as clear, and vivid, as what I now see and hear—it was a reality."

"And what *did* you see and hear?" urged his companion.

"When I awakened from the swoon I fell into on seeing *him*," said Barton, continuing as if he had not heard the question, "it was slowly, very slowly—I was reclining by the margin of a broad lake, surrounded by misty hills, and a soft, melancholy, rose-coloured light illuminated it all. It was unusually sad and lonely, and yet more beautiful than any earthly scene. My head was leaning on the lap of a girl, and she was singing a strange and wondrous song, that told, I know not how—whether by words or harmonies—of all my life—all that is past, and all that is still to come; and with the song the old feelings that I thought had perished within me came back, and tears flowed from my eyes—partly for the song and its mysterious beauty, and partly for the unearthly sweetness of her voice; yet I knew the voice—oh! how well; and I was spell-bound as I listened and looked at the strange and solitary scene, without stirring, almost without breathing—and, alas! alas! without turning my eyes toward the face that I knew was near me, so sweetly powerful was the enchantment that held me. And so, slowly and softly, the song and scene grew fainter, and ever fainter, to my senses, till all was dark and still again. And then I wakened to this world, as you saw, comforted, for I knew that I was forgiven much." Barton wept again long and bitterly.

From this time, as we have said, the prevailing tone of his mind was one of profound and tranquil melancholy. This, however, was not without its interruptions. He was thoroughly impressed with the conviction that he was to experience another and a final visitation, illimitably transcending in horror all he had before experienced. From this anticipated and unknown agony, he often shrunk in such paroxysms of abject terror and distraction, as filled the whole household with dismay and superstitious panic. Even those among them who affected to discredit the supposition of preternatural agency in the matter, were often in their secret souls visited during the darkness and solitude of night with qualms and apprehensions, which they would not have readily confessed; and none of them attempted to dissuade Barton from the resolution on which he now systematically acted, of shutting himself up in his own apartment. The window-blinds of this room were kept jealously down; and his own man was seldom out of his presence, day or night, his bed being placed in the same chamber.

This man was an attached and respectable servant; and his duties, in addition to those ordinarily imposed upon *valets*, but which Barton's independent habits generally dispensed with, were to attend carefully to the simple precautions by means of which his master hoped to exclude the dreaded recurrence of the "Watcher", as the strange letter he had at first received had designated his persecutor. And, in addition to attending to these arrangements, which consisted merely in anticipating the possibility of his master's being, through any unscreened window or opened door, exposed to the dreaded influence, the valet was never to suffer him to be for one moment alone: total solitude, even for a minute, had become to him now almost as intolerable as the idea of going abroad into the public ways—it was like some instinctive anticipation of what was coming.

It is needless to say, that under these mysterious and horrible circumstances, no steps were taken toward the fulfilment of that engagement into which he had entered. There was quite disparity enough in point of years, and indeed of habits, between the young lady and Captain Barton, to have precluded anything like very vehement or romantic attachment on her part. Though grieved and anxious, therefore, she was very far from being heart-broken; a circumstance which, for the sentimental purposes of our tale, is much to be deplored. But truth must be told, especially in a narration, whose chief, if not only, pretensions to interest consist in a rigid adherence to facts, or what are so reported to have been.

Miss Montague, however, devoted much of her time to a patient but fruitless attempt to cheer the unhappy invalid. She read for him, and conversed with him; but it was apparent that whatever exertions he made, the endeavour to escape from the one constant and ever present fear that preyed upon him was utterly and miserably unavailing.

Young ladies are much given to the cultivation of pets; and among those who shared the favour of Miss Montague was a fine old owl, which the gardener, who caught him napping among the ivy of a ruined stable, had dutifully presented to that young lady.

The caprice which regulates such preferences was manifested in the extravagant favour with which this grim and ill-favoured bird was at once distinguished by his mistress;

and, trifling as this whimsical circumstance may seem, I am forced to mention it, inasmuch as it is connected, oddly enough, with the concluding scene of the story. Barton, so far from sharing in this liking for the new favourite, regarded it from the first with an antipathy as violent as it was utterly unaccountable. Its very vicinity was unsupportable to him. He seemed to hate and dread it with a vehemence absolutely laughable, and which, to those who have never witnessed the exhibition of antipathies of this kind, would seem all but incredible.

With these few words of preliminary explanation, I shall proceed to state the particulars of the last scene in this strange series of incidents. It was almost two o'clock one winter's night, and Barton was, as usual at that hour, in his bed; the servant we have mentioned occupied a smaller bed in the same room, and a light was burning. The man was on a sudden aroused by his master, who said—

"I can't get it out of my head that that accursed bird has escaped somehow, and is lurking in some corner of the room. I have been dreaming of him. Get up, Smith, and look about; search for him. Such hateful dreams!"

The servant rose, and examined the chamber, and while engaged in so doing, he heard the well-known sound, more like a long-drawn gasp than a hiss, with which these birds from their secret haunts affright the quiet of the night. This ghostly indication of its proximity—for the sound proceeded from the passage upon which Barton's chamber-door opened—determined the search of the servant, who, opening the door, proceeded a step or two forward for the purpose of driving the bird away. He had, however, hardly entered the lobby, when the door behind him slowly swung to under the impulse, as it seemed, of some gentle current of air; but as immediately over the door there was a kind of window, intended in the day-time to aid in lighting the passage, and through which at present the rays of the candle were then issuing, the valet could see quite enough for his purpose. As he advanced he heard his master—who, lying in a well-curtained bed, had not, as it seemed, perceived his exit from the room—call him by name, and direct him to place the candle on the table by his bed. The servant, who was now some way in the long passage, and not liking to raise his voice for the purpose of replying, lest he should startle the sleeping inmates of the house, began to walk hurriedly and softly back again, when, to his amazement, he heard a voice in the interior of the chamber answering calmly, and actually saw, through the window which overtopped the door, that the light was slowly shifting, as if carried across the chamber in answer to his master's call. Palsied by a feeling akin to terror, yet not unmingled with a horrible curiosity, he stood breathless and listening at the threshold, unable to summon resolution to push open the door and enter. Then came a rustling of the curtains, and a sound like that of one who in a low voice hushes a child to rest, in the midst of which he heard Barton say, in a tone of stifled horror—"Oh, God—oh, my God!" and repeat the same exclamation several times. Then ensued a silence, which again was broken by the same strange soothing sound; and at last there burst forth, in one swelling peal, a yell of agony so appalling and hideous, that, under some impulse of ungovernable horror, the man rushed to the door, and with his whole strength strove to force it open. Whether it was that, in his agitation, he had himself but imperfectly turned the handle, or that the door was really secured upon the inside, he failed to effect an entrance; and as he tugged and pushed, yell after yell rang louder and wilder through the chamber, accompanied all the while by the same hushed sounds. Actually freezing with terror, and scarce knowing what he did, the man turned and ran down the passage, wringing his hands in the extremity of horror and irresolution. At the stair-head he was encountered by General Montague, scared and eager, and just as they met the fearful sounds had ceased.

"What is it?—who—where is your master?" said Montague, with the incoherence of extreme agitation. "Has anything—for God's sake, is anything wrong?"

"Lord have mercy on us, it's all over," said the man, staring wildly towards his master's chamber. "He's dead, sir—I'm sure he's dead."

Without waiting for inquiry or explanation, Montague, closely followed by the servant, hurried to the chamber-door, turned the handle, and pushed it open. As the door yielded to his pressure, the ill-omened bird of which the servant had been in search, uttering its spectral warning, started suddenly from the far side of the bed, and flying through the door-way close over their heads, and extinguishing, in his passage, the candle which Montague carried, crashed through the skylight that overlooked the lobby, and sailed away into the darkness of the outer space.

"There it is, God bless us," whispered the man, after a breathless pause.

"Curse that bird!" muttered the general, startled by the suddenness of the apparition, and unable to conceal his discomposure.

"The candle is moved," said the man, after another breathless pause; "see, they put it by the bed."

"Draw the curtains, fellow, and don't stand gaping there," whispered Montague, sternly.

The man hesitated.

"Hold this, then," said Montague, impatiently thrusting the candlestick into the servant's hand, and himself advancing to the bed-side, he drew the curtains apart. The light of the candle, which was still burning at the bedside, fell upon a figure huddled together, and half upright, at the head of the bed. It seemed as though it had slunk back as far as the solid panelling would allow, and the hands were still clutched in the bed-clothes.

"Barton, Barton, Barton!" cried the general, with a strange mixture of awe and vehemence. He took the candle, and held it so that it shone full upon the face. The features were fixed, stern, and white; the jaw was fallen; and the sightless eyes, still open, gazed vacantly forward toward the front of the bed. "God Almighty, he's dead," muttered the general, as he looked upon this fearful spectacle. They both continued to gaze upon it in silence for a minute or more. "And cold, too," whispered Montague, withdrawing his hand from that of the dead man.

"And see, see—may I never have life, sir," added the man, after another pause, with a shudder, "but there was something else on the bed with him. Look there—look there—see that, sir."

As the man thus spoke, he pointed to a deep indenture, as if caused by a heavy pressure, near the foot of the bed.

Montague was silent.

"Come, sir, come away, for God's sake," whispered the man, drawing close up to him, and holding fast by his arm, while he glanced fearfully round; "what good can be done here now—come away, for God's sake!"

At this moment they heard the steps of more than one approaching, and Montague, hastily desiring the servant to arrest their progress, endeavoured to loose the rigid gripe with which the fingers of the dead man were clutched in the bed-clothes, and drew, as well as he was able, the awful figure into a reclining posture; then closing the curtains carefully upon it, he hastened himself to meet those persons that were approaching.

It is needless to follow the personages so slightly connected with this narrative into the events of their after life; it is enough for us to remark, that no clue to the solution of these mysterious occurrences was ever after discovered; and so long an interval having now passed since the event which we have just described concluded this strange history, it is scarcely to be expected that time can throw any new lights upon its dark and inexplicable outline. Until the secrets of the earth shall be no longer hidden, therefore, these transactions must remain shrouded in their original impenetrable obscurity.

The only occurrence in Captain Barton's former life to which reference was ever made, as having any possible connexion with the sufferings with which his existence closed, and which he himself seemed to regard as working out a retribution for some grievous sin of his past life, was a circumstance which not for several years after his death was brought to light. The nature of this disclosure was painful to his relatives, and discreditable to his memory. As, however, we have exercised the caution of employing fictitious names; and as there are now very few living who will be able to refer to the actors in this drama, their *real* names and places in society, there is nothing to prevent our stating, in two or three lines, the substance of this discovery.

It appeared, then, that some six years before Captain Barton's final return to Dublin, he had formed, in the town of Plymouth, a guilty attachment, the object of which was the daughter of one of the ship's crew under his command. The father had visited the frailty of his unhappy child with extreme harshness, and even brutality, and it was said that she had died heart-broken. Presuming upon Barton's implication in her guilt, this man had conducted himself toward him with marked insolence, and Barton retaliated this, and what he resented with still more exasperated bitterness—his treatment of the unfortunate girl—by a systematic exercise of those terrible and arbitrary severities which the regulations of the navy placed at the command of those who are responsible for its discipline. The man had at length made his escape, while the vessel was in port at Lisbon, but died, as it was said, in an hospital in that town, of the wounds inflicted in one of his recent and sanguinary punishments.

Whether these circumstances in reality bear, or not, upon the occurrences of Barton's after-life, it is, of course, impossible to say. It seems, however, more than probable that they were, at least in his own mind, closely associated with them. But however the truth may be, as to the origin and motives of this mysterious persecution, there can be no doubt that, with respect to the agencies by which it was accomplished, absolute and impenetrable mystery is like to prevail until the day of doom.

The Fatal Bride

Being the Second Contribution
from the Reminiscences of a Bachelor

I perceive, indeed, with complacency, that you have admitted my former contribution to a place in your November number; this has determined me to despatch another, which, with like encouragement, may be followed by a third, and so on; I, all the while, with your good leave, maintaining my incognito, and despatching my scribblings through that mysterious agency, the penny-post. Should you cease to hear from me, without sufficient apparent cause for the suspension of my correspondence; should, I say, this series—for such, with your permission, I mean to make it—be abruptly and finally cut short, why then you may conclude that the "brief candle," in whose flickering light I ply this my self-imposed task, has at last gone out, and left your old and unknown correspondent to the darkness and repose to which time is hurrying us all.

With these few preliminary remarks, now offered once for all, I shall end the tedious task of introduction, and plunge at once into the business of my story, merely reiterating, by way of supplemental caution, that names and titles, and a few details of locality, which I fancied might indicate individuals, and lead to detection, have been suppressed and altered; but that in the substance, and, indeed, with those exceptions, in all the minor details of these narratives, I shall observe a strict adherence to the facts, as they were either related to me, or came within my own personal knowledge.

The story which I am about to relate, carries me back somewhere about half a century; at which time, it is needless to say, Dublin was, in point of society, a very different city from what it now is. It had then a resident aristocracy, and one whose equipages and housekeeping were maintained upon a scale which put plebeian competition wholly out of the question. I do not mean to offer any ungracious reflections upon the existing state of Dublin society. We have now, alas! more tuft-hunters than tufts to boast of; magnificent pretensions, based, like the Brahmin's world, nobody can exactly say upon what, strive and strain to fill the void, which a legitimate aristocracy have left; and men, whose grandfathers—but what matters it? the thing is after all but natural. What was a metropolis, is a capital no longer; and it is but lost time sighing after the things that once were, or snarling at those that are.

At the time of which I speak, there resided in Dublin a certain worthy baronet, whom I shall call Sir Arthur Chadleigh. He was then considerably past sixty, and was a venerable monument of what was called hard living, in all its departments. He had been, until gout disabled him, a knowing gentleman on the turf; he was a deep player and a deep drinker, and covered, with an exterior of boisterous jollity, a very cold and selfish heart. He was thoroughly a man of the world, and what was then an essential ingredient in that amiable character, whenever occasion prompted, a very determined duellist. Whatever good nature he was possessed of, was expended upon society at large. In his dealings with his own family, he was arbitrary and severe; and if he did possess any natural affections, he had managed to get them all admirably under control, and never was known, under any circumstances to suffer from their over-indulgence. This old gentleman had been blessed, in his prime, with an helpmate; but Lady Chadleigh, having been, in her own way, about as domestic a person as Sir Arthur, one fine morning, at three o'clock precisely, when her spouse was entering upon his fourth bottle of claret in the parlour, absconded with young Lord Kildalkin. The happy pair were overtaken at Havre by the baronet, who, at ten paces, duly measured, shot off Kildalkin's thumb—a feat which satisfied his honour, as some of the sterner brethren of the hair-trigger averred, at much too reasonable a rate. The worthy baronet, however, on his return, explained satisfactorily to a select circle of friends. "For," said he, "had I shot him through the head, I should not have known what the —— to do with Lady C." As it was, he left his wife in the hands of his rival, as a moderate equivalent for the joint.

Lady Chadleigh had not been cruel enough to leave her lord without some objects on which to exercise those domestic virtues, for which he was so justly celebrated. She had been just five years married, when she took her departure, as I have stated; and she left behind her, for the consolation of her spouse, along with an extensive assortment of macaws, avadavats, lap-dogs, and other sundries, three children—two sons and a girl. The macaws, &c., were easily disposed of, but there was no getting rid of the children; so Sir Arthur called in a grim old spinster sister, who, for fourteen years, dating from that day, presided at the baronet's tea-table, and ruled his little flock. At the end of this period she died, and much about the same time died also the unfortunate Lady Chadleigh, forsaken and heart-broken, in some obscure town in France.

Lady Chadleigh's name had been proscribed—in Sir Arthur's presence none dared to mention it; and, with the exception of little Mary, the daughter who, since infancy, had never seen her, no human being appeared to feel the smallest concern about the event. Little Mary Chadleigh, however, felt it deeply; with the yearnings of unavailing affection, she had always clung to the idea, that some time or other her mother would come back, and be fond of her. The reasons of the separation were, of course, wholly unknown to her, and her childish eagerness to learn something of her mother, had been systematically repulsed with a mysterious discouragement, in which she had come gradually to acquiesce. But though she had long learned to look upon her mother's absence as in some way a necessary and unavoidable privation, and even as a natural thing, and a matter of course, which scarcely required to be accounted for, yet her mind had been constantly busied with the one thought, that at last she would return, and love her as she wished to be loved. And now came these strange tidings, never looked for in her childish dreams, and these black dresses, to tell her that all the little plans and hopes that had silently fluttered her innocent heart so many a time for so many years, must end for ever; that the being for whose return she had been watching and wishing ever since she could remember, was never to come again. This was a sore shock to the poor girl, and she wept, in the solitude of her chamber, over this, to her, most bitter calamity, with a vehemence of grief and a sense of desolation, which, to one unacquainted with the cherished reveries, the castle-building of the heart, which had been her secret happiness from earliest childhood, would have been unaccountable.

Years passed on—new objects and associations began to fill her reveries; her secret sorrow wore away, and this early grief became but a sad, and scarcely unpleasing remembrance. I was a very young man when first I saw Miss Chadleigh, and I have seldom been so much struck by any combination of beauty, grace, and expression, as when she entered the room at one of Lady ——'s balls. She was at this time about nineteen, beautifully formed, and with the bearing of natural nobility; her complexion was clear, and rather pale; her eyes dark and lustrous; and her features, as I thought, exquisitely beautiful. The prevailing expression of her face was melancholy, with perhaps some slight character of haughtiness; but when she smiled, there was such a rippling of dimples, such an arch merriment in her lovely eyes, and such a revelation of little, even, pearly teeth, as made her perfectly enchanting. "Well," thought I, as I watched with absolute fascination the movements of this lovely being, "if beauty the most enchanting be any longer the potent influence it once was, there is no scheme of ambition to whose realization such loveliness as yours may not aspire." How little did I dream of what was coming!

I was so much attracted—my interest and attention so irresistibly engaged, by this beautiful girl, that I observed her, with scarcely any intermission, during the entire evening. It would he ridiculous to say that I was actually in love; I was not absurd or romantic enough (which you will) to get up a sentimental and hopeless passion at a moment's notice, and that, too, without having exchanged one word with the object of my aspirations. No such thing. The feeling with which I gazed on Miss Chadleigh, was one of the profoundest admiration, I admit, yet untinctured with any, the least, admixture of actual tenderness. I observed her with the deep and silent pleasure with which beauty of the highest order may be contemplated, without the smallest danger to the heart; and, indeed, of the philosophical nature of my admiration, I had full assurance in the fact, that I remarked, with hardly one flutter of jealousy, the attentions, evidently not ill-received, which were devotedly paid her by a singularly handsome young officer, in a perfectly irresistible cavalry uniform. This gentleman was the afterwards too-celebrated Captain Jennings.

That evening remains impressed upon my memory with the vividness—what do I say?—with fifty times the vividness of yesterday. I think I see old Sir Arthur now, and he sat at the whist-table, with his crutch beside him—for gout had claimed him as its own—his fiery face and heavy brows, overcast with the profound calculations of his favourite game, and his massive frame, shaking all over with the stentorian chuckle with which he greeted the conclusion of each successful rubber, while he slyly pocketed the guineas, and rallied and quizzed his discomfited opponents, with ferocious good-humour. I looked at this old man with some curiosity. I had never seen him before, and in his past life were not a few passages of vicissitude, daring, and adventure, such as might well warrant that qualified degree of interest which, as a young man, I not unnaturally felt in him. As I observed this hero of a hundred stories in the gossip of the day—his massive, but now crippled form—his bloated face, in which few could have traced a vestige of the handsome traits which rumour assigned to his early youth, and upon which, in the intervals of his tempestuous good-humour, I thought I could clearly discover the stamp of those sterner and imperious attributes with which general report had invested him;—as I looked on this fierce, crafty, intemperate, but at the same time, strangely enough, by no means unpopular man of the world, it was impossible to avoid the trite but natural contrast which, in a thousand such cases, is forced upon the mind, as often as, turning from him, my eye rested upon his beautiful child. How could a creature so exquisitely lovely, so accomplished in every natural grace—and, if expression might be trusted, at once so refined, so noble, and so sensitive—have ever sprung from a root so gnarled, bitter, and unsightly! Yet his child she doubtless was; for the world, with all its jealous and censorious curiosity, had never once questioned the parentage of Sir Arthur's children, and in this the world was right. For poor Lady Chadleigh had begun her married life a good and faithful wife, and under circumstances less unhappy, might have been pure and honoured to the last. But the insults of callous profligacy had alienated and exasperated a heart at once proud and impetuous. She had been a spoiled child, and became a ruined woman. Habitually ungoverned, she was incapable of forbearance. With little principle and less prudence, she suffered a restless sense of wrong to hurry her into extravagances of conduct—intended, but without effect, to pique Sir Arthur, and wound at least his pride into jealousy; and in this mad enterprise the unhappy woman had at last effectually compromised herself, and was forced to the terrible necessity of flight. Her fall was not that of an impure, but of a vengeful spirit. It was the act of a bitter and passionate suicide, who would squander fifty lives to bring home one pang of remorse, or any other feeling, to the heart of callous indifference. Poor thing! the world understood her character, and despised her; for want of a due contempt for Sir Arthur's apathy, and a proper acquiescence in his profligate courses, she had given herself to ruin.

"Who is that officer," I asked a friend, whom accident brought close to me in the crowded room—"that good-looking fellow, who has been so marked in his devotions to Miss Chadleigh all the evening?"

"Oh! that—don't you know?" he replied. "Why that is Captain Jennings—Jennings the aid-de-camp—a devilish handsome fellow; the women are quite mad about him, and he knows it."

"Miss Chadleigh appears intimate with him," I observed.

"Yes, so she is; he was a friend of young Chadleigh's, who died, or was taken in some battle in India," he answered.

"So, one of her brothers is dead, then?" I interrupted.

"Yes; I believe the native army made him a prisoner, and treated him in the usual way," replied he. "I heard the particulars; they were deuced horrid; but I don't quite recollect them now."

"And, Miss Chadleigh—has not she a second brother?" I inquired.

"A second brother! Yes," he answered. "A pleasant fellow; but a perfect devil for wildness. She was fond of the other brother, and in a sad way, I believe, when the news came; but that is a year and a-half since. There, now, you can see young Chadleigh—the young man going to take Miss Chadleigh away."

He nodded to indicate the party, and I followed the direction of his eye.

Young Chadleigh was a decidedly well-looking man, with a frank and rather distinguished air, and dressed with an almost foppish attention to the prevailing fashion. I had just time to observe that he and Jennings chatted familiarly for a minute or two, and appeared to be on the friendliest terms of intimacy.

"Well," thought I, "after all, he may be but a friend."

Whether it be impossible to contemplate such beauty as Miss Chadleigh's with perfect stoicism, and that, without knowing it, I was really a little jealous, I can't say; but I certainly had watched the young captain's attentions with a slight but disagreeable sense of restlessness, and experienced, I know not how, a certain relief in the reflection I had just made. It had, however, hardly visited my mind, when it was again disturbed.

Miss Chadleigh, leaning on her brother's arm, was passing so close as almost to touch me, whom she had unconsciously inspired with so much admiration, when Jennings, following, presented her with her fan, accidentally forgotten. As she took it with a gracious smile, she blushed. Yes, I could not be mistaken, for a more beautiful blush I never beheld in my existence; and, to make the matter worse, I thought I perceived that, as he placed the light weapon of coquetry in her hand, his own rested upon her's for a second longer than was strictly necessary, and in doing so conveyed the slightest possible pressure to her little ivory fingers. I felt, I know not how, disposed to be affronted and incensed, and actually stared, with no very inviting expression, full upon Captain Jennings, as he made his retreat, with a lurking smile of vanity and triumph on his lip. My ill-bred stare was unobserved, and I could, on reflection, scarcely help laughing at the absurdity of the emotion which had inspired it. But, after all, why should I?—the nature of the beast pervades us all. The presence of beauty is a woeful stimulus to unprovoked combativeness, and I do believe there is a lurking idea universally in the mind of man, that beauty should be, somehow, the prize of the fiercest and strongest—the

"Viribus editior ut in grege taurus."

I know it was ever the case with me—I never saw, at least in my young days, a pretty girl, without feeling a disposition to fight with somebody—and this, although, under ordinary circumstances, as peaceable a fellow as any among her majesty's liege subjects.

In pursuing this narrative, I am forced occasionally to rely upon the report of others; in some of its oddest scenes, however, as the reader will perceive, I was present, and myself a secondary actor. What I did not myself witness, I shall, as I have said, supply from the testimony of others, and thus present your readers with a connected recital of this eccentric piece of Irish biography.

If fortune had condemned Captain Jennings to the torments of love, she was, at all events, resolved to grant him every reasonable mitigation in his distressed condition. For upwards of a month, during that summer, he had the happiness of being a guest at Lord ———'s, where Miss Chadleigh and her brother were also visitors; whether he had succeeded, or not, in making any impression upon the young lady's heart, was not then known; but as his attentions were, if possible, more marked and devoted than ever, the affair began to be talked of, and, soon after this visit terminated, was mentioned by a friend to Sir Arthur himself.

The baronet forthwith instituted inquiries respecting Captain Jennings' ways and means—the result was unsatisfactory—and, one day, as the gay young gentleman sat chatting, at an early visit, with Chadleigh and his fair sister, the old baronet hobbled into the room, and set himself down as one of the party—a procedure quite contrary to his ordinary habits. There was nothing ominous in his countenance and bearing, however; on the contrary, he seemed more than usually frank and good-humoured, shook Jennings more heartily by the hand, and laughed more boisterously at all his jokes and stories than ever he had done before. Chadleigh had already gone, and Sir Arthur having dispatched Mary to superintend some customary arrangements affecting his own comforts, the door was closed upon him and Captain Jennings.

"Jennings," said the baronet.

"Well, sir."

"You're a devilish good fellow—Jennings, a devilish pleasant fellow," said the baronet, "and I've no doubt will get on in the world—with prudence, that is, with prudence."

Jennings bowed his acknowledgments, and looked a little surprised.

"And, as it strikes me, Jennings, my boy," continued the baronet, in the same jolly tone—"about the most imprudent thing you could possibly do, at the outset would be to marry; and marriage being out of the question in point of prudence—totally and entirely out of the question—I should not, you understand me, like to have Miss Chadleigh, my daughter, talked of in connexion with such an absurdity."

"Really, Sir Arthur," interrupted Jennings, changing colour slightly, and affecting a cool hauteur, which he was far from feeling—"I don't precisely know to what particular circumstances you are pleased to allude."

"Come, come, my dear fellow," said Sir Arthur, in the same tone of rough good humour, which, in all his dealings, alike with friend or foe, whether with the dice-box or the pistol, he had ever maintained—"we are, both of us, men of the world—eh? I an old, and you a young one; but both of us unquestionably men of the world, and perfectly wide awake. You know just as well as I, and I as well as you, what is usually termed, paying attentions to a young lady—let us have no shamming at either side—we both of us know this; and I don't approve of Miss Chadleigh's receiving any such distinction from you, my dear Jennings; and now I hope I have made myself perfectly intelligible."

Jennings bowed stiffly, and the baronet continued—

"A set of meddling old women have begun to talk, you see, and I took this, the earliest opportunity, of putting you on your guard—for, of course, it would not answer your cards either, to have such nonsense put about, and so, without anything abrupt or remarkable, your acquaintance must become cooler, and—and—more distant; and, in short, when you do happen to meet in society, the less you are thrown together, the better; in a word, my dear Jennings, your coolness must effectually give the lie to this ridiculous piece of gossip."

As Sir Arthur concluded, he was slowly rising from his seat, and having, just at its termination, established his ponderous and gouty person in an erect position, he took Jennings' hands in both his, and shaking them very cordially, said, in precisely the tone which might have conveyed a hospitable and pressing invitation—

"And, by the way, my dear Jennings, I think it would be very advisable, don't you, by way of a beginning, to put an immediate stop to these little visits—these foolish little morning calls, which make people talk, and serve no possible purpose, as matters stand, except as a very unnecessary tax upon your time; so, for the future"—here he renewed the shaking, with increasing warmth—"when we do meet, let it be abroad, my dear Jennings, and not here; you understand me, not on any account here; in society, of course, I shall always be delighted to meet you; we shall there, of course, be the best possible friends; and now, my dear Jennings, I think we perfectly understand one another, and I'll not waste any more of your time, for, of course, you have many more amusing ways of employing it. Good morning, Jennings, my boy—farewell."

The perfect radiation of cordiality and good humour with which this very peremptory dismissal was conveyed, was so incongruously disconcerting, that Jennings felt totally unable to resent the procedure as he felt disposed to do—for, truth to say, he was more nettled than he cared to confess, even to himself. Returning the old gentleman's salutation, therefore, stiffly and coldly enough, he withdrew, and had walked nearly half-way along the side of St. Stephen's-green (in the immediate neighbourhood of which Sir Arthur resided) before he began to recover the angry confusion of this affronting congé. Slackening his pace, however, he began to revolve the occurrences in his mind, and, with the resignation of necessity, began to discover many things to be grateful for among the consequences of this explanation, brusque and unexpected as it undoubtedly was.

"Well, well," he muttered, "it is, perhaps, much better as it is. She is a devilish fine girl, to be sure, and, I do believe, had well nigh turned my head; but, egad, I was acting like a fool—a —— fool, to follow her about, and get myself entangled at all—heaven knows what an infernal piece of mischief it might have ended in, if I had been left to my own foolish fancies—I'm a deuced deal a happier man, as matters stand—a safer one, at all events."

Jennings was a singularly handsome young man, as we have said—very vain and very selfish; he knew no control except that involved in a punctilious subservience to the code of fashionable society in which he lived; and, without any one grain of positive malevolence in his disposition, he had about him a great deal of the raw material out of which circumstances and opportunity might eventually fabricate a villain; an inconsiderate impetuosity, too often mistaken for generosity and impulsive candour; an exacting and ambitious vanity, which, ever seeking for new homage, inspired a constant desire to please— and, with the desire, stimulated the constant practice, too, of all the little arts of pleasing—and which, however despicable a passion in itself, was yet, in its effects, the prime cause of his popularity—these, combined with a constitutional selfishness which instinctively governed all his views and actions, were the leading attributes of a character—unfortunately for the dignity of human nature—commonplace enough. Externally, however, he was a very fascinating person—accomplished, elegant, agreeable, and blessed with an inexhaustible flow of gay and sparkling spirits.

Of course, it was to be presumed that Sir Arthur had conveyed to Miss Chadleigh his views respecting Jennings' attentions; and the baronet's stern and implacable severity in punishing disobedience, and enforcing compliance with his commands, was so thoroughly known and understood, that not one of his children dared openly to disobey his lightest order. Mary Chadleigh and Jennings, however, were destined often to meet—indeed it could not be otherwise, unless one or other of them had withdrawn from that gay society in which both of them mixed so freely. There was, however, a very marked change in their mutual demeanour. There was an obvious reserve on her part; though ill-natured people observed that her eyes were oftener seen following his movements in the crowded saloons than was either to be accounted for by pure accident, or altogether reconcilable with the show of coldness with which she now habitually met him. On his part, the change was also marked; instead of devoting his attentions and his time, as heretofore, whenever fortune brought them together, all but exclusively to her, he now scarcely ever exchanged a dozen sentences with her; in short, though the female world good-naturedly persisted in believing Miss Chadleigh a very ill-used, and, spite of her assumed indifference, a very devoted damsel—yet all were agreed that this affair was totally and finally at an end.

It was not very long until gossip began to busy itself once more with this young lady's name—a new suitor began to be suspected. Young Lord Dungarret, with a coronet and twelve thousand a-year at his disposal, was evidently smitten, and to such a degree, that Miss Chadleigh became ten degrees more ugly than ever in the eyes of the female world of Dublin. While matters were in this state, however, it happened that one day, as Sir Arthur sate in his chamber, damning his old enemy, the gout, in solitary suffering and ill-temper, somebody hesitatingly knocked at his chamber door.

"Come in—well?" he exclaimed, turning his mottled and gloomy visage full on the intruder.

The person who entered was old Martha, a privileged domestic of some three-score years, who had been the nurse, and was now the attendant of Mary Chadleigh, whom she absolutely idolized. "I'm come, sir, about the young mistress," she said, approaching; "for, indeed, I'm afraid she's very bad—she's very sick, sir, and I would not be easy without the doctor seeing her."

"Sick—is she?" said the baronet; "young ladies are always ailing—it's interesting, and nurses always croaking— they have nothing else to do; I wish she had half-a-day's experience of my gout—curse it—and she'd know what pain is like."

"Why, then, indeed, sir, she really is bad, and very bad, I'm afraid, this time," said the woman, with dignified emphasis. "It is not, of course, for an old woman like me, that's nothing to the darling young lady, more than just nursing her and taking care of her, to be dictating to her own father, that, of course, has more feeling for his own child than the likes of me 'id have; but all I say is, she is really bad, and—"

"Well, well, well—send for the doctor, to be sure, and don't plague me any more; and just tell him," he added, as the old woman reached the door, "if he finds anything seriously amiss, that I will feel much obliged by his looking in here, and telling me what he thinks of her—do you hear?"

In obedience to the summons, accordingly dispatched, Dr. Robertson, as I shall call him, then in extensive practice in Dublin, and who had been for twenty years the physician in attendance upon the family, arrived late in the evening. He was a large, good-natured man, with a rough voice, emphatic delivery, and a brusque and decisive manner—clear-headed and rapid—with a thorough knowledge of the world, as well as a consummate skill in his profession. With a very rough exterior, and an occasional coarseness, and even severity of expression, Dr. Robertson was, nevertheless, a kind and tender-hearted man; and these sterling qualities had served to secure him a vested interest in the practice to which his reputation had once introduced him.

It was, as I have said, late in the evening, when a peremptory double knock at the door announced the arrival of the physician. With brisk and creaking steps he followed the servant, who conducted him directly to the young lady's chamber. The house was a vast and handsome mansion; and after ascending a stone staircase, and passing a handsome lobby, he found himself in a kind of antechamber, from which the young lady's sleeping apartment opened. Here he remained for a moment, while old Martha went in to prepare her young mistress for the visit. After about a minute, she returned, and intimated that Miss Chadleigh was ready.

Doctor Robertson accordingly entered. The young lady was lying upon her bed, her face deadly pale, except where two bright spots of hectic crimson glowed with unnatural warmth; her eyes were swollen with tears, and as the physician approached, she turned away from his well-known, good-natured countenance, and hid her face in the bedclothes.

"Well, well, my dear, what is all this? Come, come, we'll make a cure of you in no time—don't fret—we'll have you well in a day or two."

Thus saying, in rough and kindly tones, he took her hand, and as he felt her pulse, continued—

"And tell me where you feel amiss—there's a good child—don't sob—don't cry—I promise you it won't signify."

"Oh, doctor," she said, with her face still averted, "I am very ill, and—and—in such wretched spirits."

Here the poor girl again burst into tears; and while she was weeping, the old nurse stole noiselessly out of the chamber, and closing the door, walked restlessly from one spot to another in the outer room we have described; now arranging a screen, now replacing a chair by the wall, now stirring the fire, but, with an abstracted and miserable look, and wringing her withered bands ever and anon in the intervals. This had gone on with little variation, except that the old woman occasionally looked with an expression of intense anxiety, and even horror, at the door which concealed her young mistress and her professional visitor from view, when at last it opened, and Doctor Robertson came out, buried, as it seemed, in profound and painful thought, and looking unusually pale and agitated; he walked, by two or three steps at a time, pausing, and occasionally shaking his head gloomily in the intervals, and sate himself down in silence before the fire, and ruminated for some minutes. At last he stood up briskly, turned his back to the fire, beckoned to the old woman, and as she approached, raised the candle, so that its light fell full upon her face.

"Where do you sleep, Martha?" he asked, abruptly.

"Where—where do I sleep?" she echoed, stammeringly.

"Ay, ma'am, where?" he repeated, sternly.

"Why—why here, sir, here in this room," she answered, with some confusion.

He fixed his eyes upon her sharply for a few seconds, and then as abruptly said—

"And how does your mistress rest at night, pray?"

"She rests—she rests—why, sir, she rests pretty well, sir; but why do you ask me?"

He continued to regard the old woman with the same steady scrutiny for some seconds; at last she said, with an affronted air, and rather an effort, for she was, whatever the cause might be, very much disconcerted—

"I'm sure I don't know, sir, what you're looking at me that way for; a body 'id think I was took for a thief."

"There—there—never mind," he said, putting down the candle; "no offence, nurse, no offence—go in to your young mistress. Is there—ay, there's pen and ink here— very well—just go in, and I'll call you when I want you."

Accordingly, the old woman, muttering and sniffing, hobbled into the adjoining room, and closed the door, unaccountably, as it seemed, both irritated and alarmed.

Doctor Robertson being left alone, leaned, in deep re- flection, for a minute or two upon the mantel-piece; he then glanced round the room, and observing another door in it, he walked over, opened it, and looked out. It com- manded a landing-place upon a back staircase.

"Ha!" said he, as he closed the door, and returned to the fireplace, whistling slowly, and with rather a dismal countenance, a few interrupted staves as he went, he sat down, and after a brief pause exclaimed—

"Poor thing!—poor thing!—it must not rest here. Dear me—dear me—how very strange—I must see her again— humph!—perplexing, but—ay, ay—I'll see her again—it is much better."

So saying, he called Martha, gave her some general directions about preparing slops, &c., and telling her to attend to these arrangements meanwhile, he once more entered his patient's chamber.

It was fully half-an-hour afterwards, that Dr. Robertson knocked at Sir Arthur Chadleigh's door.

"Poor little thing!" said he, after a few introductory sentences, exchanged at either side, "she is seriously indisposed, feverish, and very nervous, and, I fear, without an immediate prospect of complete recovery. The best thing to be done for her is, to keep her from all excitement and agitation; her hours must be early, and the fewer visitors she sees the better. In short, I have spoken to her very fully; she is now in possession of my opinion, and appears perfectly disposed to follow my directions implicitly, so there is little else to be done for the present, than to permit her to do as she herself shall desire. In the meantime, I will look in from time to time, to see that all goes on well."

"And pray, Doctor Robertson, how soon may we expect her perfect restoration to health," said Sir Arthur, and with a coarse chuckle he added, "for egad, if a girl is to marry at all, it won't do to have her locked up long—there's no time like the present, my dear sir, especially in the case of youth and good looks."

"True, Sir Arthur; very true," said the medical man; "but, in Miss Chadleigh's case, it would not be safe to undertake her recovery within any limited time—she may possibly be well in a few weeks, and possibly not for a year; it is impossible to predict with certainty; it is one of those doubtful cases, which may go on for a very long time, and which, at the same time, may just as possibly take a good or an ill turn within a fortnight."

"It's cursed provoking—the dear child!" ejaculated Sir Arthur, petulantly, as he thought of Lord Dungarret and his twelve thousand a-year—"what do you say to a week or so in the country?"

"Umph! I proposed that; but she did not like it," said Doctor Robertson; "and her disliking it would make the experiment mischievous instead of useful: her nerves are as much affected as her general health; so that we must not contradict her fancies, or irritate her on any account; she must be allowed to choose for herself—except in matters of essential importance; and in those she has good sense enough to defer implicitly to her medical adviser; so I shall look in, from time to time, and see that matters go on properly, and report progress to you accordingly."

With these words he took his leave. As Doctor Robertson was in large and fashionable practice, Miss Chadleigh's illness was soon generally known; some said it was merely a ruse to complete the reduction of Lord Dungarret; others, that she was broken-hearted for love of the faithless Captain Jennings; many pitied her, and some few sincerely lamented her absence.

I recollect, about this time, strolling into the theatre one evening with two or three acquaintances. We took our places in the back of a box, in the next one to which I observed Jennings. One of my party happened to be acquainted with him, and the following conversation passed between them—a conversation which indirectly threw a light upon some of the darkest passages of his subsequent history—

"I say, Jennings, did you hear the news about the Chadleighs?"

"No—what news?" he inquired, quickly.

"Why, young Chadleigh told me, not an hour since, a letter has come from his brother Dick, whom we all thought was killed and cut up in India; but far from it, he is perfectly well, and returning home on leave."

"Good God! how extraordinary!—I really am delighted to hear it!" exclaimed Jennings, growing pale, nevertheless, and looking stunned and alarmed, instead of overjoyed, as his words implied.

"He has quite a tale of wonders to tell about his escapes and all that," continued his informant; and so rattled on for a time, until, the curtain rising, he directed his attention to the stage.

Though Jennings immediately recovered his serenity of countenance, he grew silent, and in a few minutes withdrew from the theatre, leaving, in my mind at least, impressions not very favourable to the strength of his affections or the value of his friendship. I did not then know the positive reasons which he had for dreading his young friend's return.

Time wore on—months passed away—still Doctor Robertson responded, with gloomy uncertainty, to the inquiries with which he was assailed from all sides; and the general impression began to be, that poor Miss Chadleigh's recovery was becoming at least a very doubtful contingency. Such was the posture of affairs, when your humble servant, who pens these pages, was himself involved in an adventure which it is necessary here to detail.

I had left a pleasant party, somewhere about one o'clock at night, and, without having positively transgressed the limits of sobriety, I had taken just wine enough to predispose me to embark in any exciting enterprise which might torn up. I was quite alone; and, as the reader is probably aware, the streets of Dublin were by no means so safe at night-time in the period of which I speak, as they now are; but relying upon the sword, which the fashion of those days made a necessary appendage, and in whose use I was a tolerably accomplished proficient, I rather courted than avoided such adventures as chance might possibly present. And in this spirit, instead of pursuing the open streets, I threaded the narrow alleys and back lanes with a careless sort of swagger, and a pugnacious disposition, the very remembrance of which, even at this time of day, makes me blush for the reckless folly of my youth. The perversity of fortune was, however, in this instance, as in many others, apparent—silence and solitude encountered my advance. I was now just entering, in my devious ramble, a dingy stable-lane, whose entire length was enlivened by but three twinkling oil-lamps, whose dusky radiance scarcely extended a yard around the wooden posts that supported them. This dismal and silent alley ran immediately behind the west-side of St. Stephen's-green; and I observed the figure of a man walking up and down, as it seemed to me, with cautious and suspicious tread. I could perceive nothing of him, however, in the dusky light, except that, as he passed and repassed immediately under one of the lamps, its faint rays fell upon a broad-brimmed hat, and a great-coat, in which the figure was enveloped. My vague suspicions were confirmed, by observing that this man withdrew himself, with cautious haste, as I advanced, and was soon lost to my sight. I was standing, still looking in the direction in which the figure had disappeared, when a little wicket, in one of the gates opening upon the lane, was drawn back close to where I stood, and a suppressed female voice inquired—

"Are you there?"

"Yes," answered I, promptly; now, for the first time, beginning to feel that an adventure was coming, and inclined to bear my part in it to the close, end how it might.

"Where?" repeated the voice.

"Here," I answered, approaching the aperture.

A female, muffled in a cloak and bonnet, was passing through the wicket, and making me a sign to draw nearer, she said, hurriedly,

"Here—take it—and then wait for us where you are."

At the same time she placed a small bundle in my hands, which I received, nothing doubting that I was innocently made a partner in some night robbery, whose true accomplice was the man whom I had seen walking to-and-fro, as I described, and for whom, doubtless, the woman had mistaken me. With a secret satisfaction at the surprise I was about to give the party, I held the parcel fast, and took a few turns, up and down, before the spot where I had received it, awaiting the further progress of the affair.

While thus engaged, I was nearly met, face to face, by the man whom I had at first seen, and who, hearing some noise, doubtless, at the appointed place of rendezvous, had hurried back. On descrying me, however, he instantly retired as before; and I, fearing to interrupt the current of the adventure, forbore in anywise to obstruct his escape. I had walked thus back and forward, bundle in hand, for eight or ten minutes, when the wicket was opened once more, and the woman I had spoken to already, stepped out into the lane, and said—

"Stand back a little bit, an' follow us, and don't for the life of you drop that."

Almost at the same time two other figures came forth, muffled as carefully as the first, and I heard a female voice from within the wicket, pouring forth, as it seemed to me, prayers and blessings, interrupted with sobs. The door was cautiously closed from the inside, and I heard the key slowly and carefully turned in the rusty lock; and as these sounds were audible, the little party began to move forward, while I, in obedience to orders, brought up the rear, carrying the parcel carefully in my arms.

The person in the centre of the three appeared to be feeble, and to advance with pain, and as she did so, leaned heavily upon the others.

Thus we proceeded, until we reached the end of this lane, and turned into another as solitary and ill-lighted. As the party before me passed under the lamp at the corner, one of the women upon whom she in the middle was leaning, exclaimed—

"Give me them, my jewel; they are better off where we are going."

And thus saying, she drew off two or three rings that glittered upon the fingers that pressed her arm, and slipped them into her pocket. This done, they relapsed into total silence, and, full of curiosity for the issue, I followed close upon their steps.

We had now walked, though very slowly, for nearly ten minutes, when, in a dark spot, close under a broad gateway, they stopped.

"Thank God, we are so far," said one of the women; "sit down on that, my darling, for a minute;" and so saying, she laid a shawl, which she folded up in the fashion of a cushion, upon the top of one of the short upright stones which protected the corners of the piers; and upon this rude seat, the silent, and, as it seemed, exhausted figure, sank down. The woman who had just accosted me, now beckoned me to her, and taking the bundle from me, said:—

"Now run down there, and bring up a chair from the stand at the second corner."

She indicated the direction with her hand, and I—exerting myself to the full, as much as if I had had a personal stake in the enterprise, in which I thus found myself, through sheer wantonness, actively involved—ran at my utmost speed upon the errand, and quickly returned with the desired conveyance.

Into this, the feeble woman who had been resting as I have described, was hurried, and the chairmen having received directions to follow the two others, and I in turn to follow them, we all trudged onward, for forty minutes and upwards, in absolute silence.

By that time we had penetrated considerably beyond Werburgh-street, and were now entering the Liberties, when turning abruptly into a short, dark, dilapidated street, the women stopped in front of a tall, dingy house, and after inspecting its exterior and interchanging a few words, they signed to the chairmen to set down their conveyance. Some one had probably been watching for its arrival, from one of the many dark windows which overlooked the street, for she who had sate in it was hardly disengaged from the chair, when the hall-door was stealthily opened, and a grimy, suspicious-looking girl, with a wretched candle in one hand, and shading her eyes with the other, peeped out.

"Give me that," said the woman who had spoken to me, and who seemed to have the command of the expedition, at the same time entering, and taking the candle from her, while she drew the door fully open.

"All right?" she added, inquiringly, glancing significantly upwards.

"Ay, everything," rejoined the other, sleepily; at the same time the other two women entered and passed silently on toward the stairs.

"Pay the men, now, and come in yourself," added the same woman, addressing me. I fortunately had about me enough change to satisfy the chairmen, which, as it seemed it was my province to do, and having dismissed them, I followed my conductress into the house, and surrendered the bundle into her bands.

She turned the key in the hall-door, and beckoned me into a dilapidated wainscotted back-room, on the window-sill of which she placed the dipt candle, which faintly lighted this inhospitable apartment, and pointing to the only piece of furniture which garnished its walls, a solitary, clumsy chair, placed there, I suppose, in anticipation of my arrival, she said—

"Wait there, my good man, till I come back by-and-bye, and you know the rest."

As she spoke to me, I for the first time saw her countenance, which was about as ugly and sinister a one as I had ever beheld; very nearly resembling the lineaments usually ascribed in fairy tales, and other such authentic records, to witches of the malignant kind; a yellow skin, hooked nose, a wide mouth, with a few carious fangs, and a marvellous prominence of chin, gave additional effect to a pair of eyes, whose fierce and rat-like vivacity seemed scarcely reconcilable with the evident antiquity of her other features; and though her head was somewhat sunk upon her chest, yet her original wiry activity seemed to have suffered little abatement from years. This woman's countenance, I confess, impressed me most unfavourably with respect to the object of these arrangements; and I could not help entertaining a vague and unpleasant suspicion of meditated foul-play, and impending mischief, as the glance of this ill-favoured hag continued to haunt my fancy long after she had left me to the dreary solitude of the apartment. There was something, perhaps, a little wounding to the self-love of a young man in being thus coolly set down, as I clearly was, for a lackey; but this I must do myself the justice to say, that I was buttoned up in a great-coat fashioned more with a view to comfort than to elegance; and provided with a hat which had seen a great deal of rough night-duty.

The interest I felt in the denouement of the adventure, however, prevented my troubling myself much about this; and seating myself, pursuant to the old woman's directions, in the solitary chair, I was left alone to keep watch in this singularly bleak and comfortless apartment.

Insensibly I began to grow sleepy; and, adjusting myself in as easy an attitude as my uncomfortable position would permit, I fell into an uneasy dose, in which the ill-looking hag, who had last left me, was in my sleeping fancy, hovering about me, and offering me share of the rings I had seen her take, on condition of my being accessary to some infernal crime, which she was always on the point of confiding to me, yet, somehow or other, never divulged, when I was startled from my dreams by a piercing cry. For a moment I forgot where I was; the sound was still ringing in my ears, and the candle, the snuff of which out-topped its blaze, afforded but an imperfect and shadowy light. Full of uneasy apprehensions, I walked softly into the hall, and made my way to the foot of the stairs, where I stood, listening breathlessly for the slightest sound of a human voice, but in vain. I thought, indeed, I could distinguish in some remote upper-room the shuffling of feet, but of this I could not, on account of the constant rattling of the old window-frames in the wind, be perfectly certain. After waiting for a considerable time, I was about to abandon my new position, or to return to my post in the parlour, when I once more distinctly heard the same piercing cry of agony which had at first startled me. Without one moment's hesitation, I drew my sword, strode by three-at-a-time up the stairs, the cries continuing as I ascended; and just as I reached the room from which they were issuing, they subsided into a moan, and I heard the tread of steps as before. I rushed directly to the door, sword in hand, and pushing it open, was some paces towards the centre of the chamber before I could arrest my advance. I had good reason to be astounded. A fire was lighted, and several wax-candles were burning in the room, and illuminated abundance of furniture, somewhat dingy to be sure, but still, as it struck me, comfortable and respectable in appearance; there were curtains carefully drawn across the windows, a carpet on the floor, and a large bed, at one side of which stood, the one a little in advance of the other, the two women I had accompanied, now divested of their bonnets and cloaks; at the other, Doctor Robertson; and in the bed itself, flushed, exhausted, and as it seemed to me, well nigh dying—heavens! could I believe it—Miss Chadleigh herself.

I stood for several moments absolutely petrified with amazement; and those upon whose offices I had thus unexpectedly intruded, in so warlike an attitude, returned my look with a gaze of scarcely less astonishment than mine. The poor young lady, who lay quite motionless, with her eyes just closed, appeared, however, wholly unconscious of the intrusion. Before I had recovered sufficiently from the stupefaction of this extraordinary discovery, Doctor Robertson had taken me roughly by the collar, and drew me, or rather pushed me out of the apartment.

In reply to his angry interrogatories, which he had suppressed until I had reached the lobby, I offered the best explanation, namely, the simple truth.

"Robbers, indeed!" he muttered—"more likely to be one of the gang yourself—"

And calling out one of the women, and having exchanged a few words in a whisper with her, I presume touching myself, he appeared satisfied, and told me to get down again as fast as I could, and to beware how I came again where I was not wanted. Sustaining as well as I could the character assigned me, as it were, by common consent, I conducted myself under this rebuke, as a respectful lackey might be supposed to do. I was so much shocked, that on reaching the chamber where I had been directed to wait, I could scarcely collect my thoughts. Only to think of Miss Chadleigh's being reduced to a situation so strange and deplorable!—she whom I had last seen the admired of all beholders—the life and the ornament of the gay and elegant society in which she moved. Merciful heaven! how repulsive, degrading, and melancholy was the contrast. A prey to a thousand conflicting and tumultuous feelings, I leaned upon the old chimney-piece, gazing into the black and empty grate, lost, not in conjecture or surmise, but in mere confusion, amazement, and, I might almost add, consternation.

While thus engaged, I was tapped on the shoulder by the old woman, whose entrance I had not perceived.

"Poor young lady!" said I—"how is she now?"

"Bad enough," said the woman—"don't you hear her?"

"Poor thing! she seems very ill, indeed!" I answered.

"Ay, ay," she repeated, with a smile, for which I could have strangled her, "it's all one, rich or poor, on that bed. She's in the hands of God now, an' nothing but Him and patience to look to—"

"God help her—God help her!" I repeated.

"Och, never a fear of her," said she, snuffing the candle with her bony fingers; and then putting her hand in her pocket, she gave me a note, saying—

"You're to bring that to him the minute the child's born; and mind, you're to tell him—for the foolish creature set her heart on it—that she wrote it the very last minute she could hold a pen, do you mind? and don't go until I come back and tell you whether it's a boy or a girl; though, God knows, I don't see much differ it makes."

With this remark she withdrew, and I, with intense curiosity, approached the candle to read the address of the billet. "Richard Hamilton Jennings, Esq.," was written with a trembling hand upon it, and, fortunately for my incognito, his address in full subscribed. I now began, for the first time, fully to appreciate the extreme awkwardness and embarrassment of the very equivocal position into which my precipitate folly had led me. I had become possessed of a secret, involving the reputations, perhaps the lives of others, and by a coincidence which, however purely accidental and unpremeditated upon my part, I yet could not help perceiving might, at the same time, expose me to the most painful and disreputable surmises and misconstruction. It was, however, too late now to extricate myself, without possibly doing still further mischief; my now withdrawing could effect no possible good; and, on the whole, I judged it best to perform the services committed to the domestic whose place I had so foolishly taken, and then to confide in Doctor Robertson (whose character, as well as his appearance, I perfectly knew, although I had no actual acquaintance with himself), the exact nature of my position in the affair, believing, and as I still think, with reason, that it would be a relief to the parties who had reason to dread being compromised, to learn that their secret accidentally divulged, had, at all events, fallen into the keeping of a gentleman and a man of honour.

I had hardly arrived at this resolution, when I heard the stealthy tread, and the uneasy respiration of the old woman on her return.

"Well, it's all over, an' a quick case it was," she murmured, as she entered. "She may well be thankful, so she may, not to be undher them, like many a poor creature that's bad fur a night and a day, and longer."

"And how is she?" I urged.

"Och, well enough—as well as can be," she answered—"right well. Don't be delaying any longer; an' don't drop the note, for the life of you. Tell him it's a boy, an' a real plentiful boy; and she's getting on elegant."

So saying, she hurried me to the hall-door, and observed in conclusion—

"Don't clap the door, do ye mind? and if you have any message back, don't knock loud—do you hear me?"

It was still profoundly dark, and the streets silent and deserted. It was past three o'clock, probably nearer four, as I knocked at Captain Jennings' lodgings. He had a handsome set of apartments in Kildare-street, and through the blinds of the drawing-room windows I could see the glare of lights, and the shadows of persons in the room. The hall, too, was lighted; and from the promptitude with which the door was opened, as well as from the talking and laughter audible from the drawing-room, as I followed the servant up the stairs, it was manifest that Captain Jennings was seeing company.

The servant was a novice in his duties I suppose; for instead of acquainting his master with my arrival, and leaving me to wait in the hall, he ushered me up at once into his presence. Perhaps, indeed, by way of compensation to my self-esteem, the worthy fellow, with more discrimination than those whom I had last encountered, detected something of the gentleman under my assumed lackeyism. In obedience to his directions, therefore, and perhaps with some lurking curiosity to witness the contrasted situation of himself and of his victim, in the self-same hour, I stepped into the room. It was light as day with wax-lights, and the party, which consisted of some eight or ten, were for the most part engaged at cards. They were all talking and laughing with noisy gaiety; and an elegant supper was laid, with a profusion of plate and wine-coolers, at a long side-table. One of the first persons I saw was young Chadleigh, who was just concluding a satirical anecdote as I entered, and the next was Jennings. I saw the latter cast an angry glance at the servant, and instantly resume the smile with which he awaited the point of young Chadleigh's story; but I plainly perceived that in spite of his command of muscle, his face had grown almost deadly pale.

He waved his hand impatiently to us to withdraw, and as I did so, I saw him fill out a glass of wine. In the midst of the buzz and laughter which followed Chadleigh's anecdote, Captain Jennings joined me in the lobby, and as he did so, I heard Chadleigh call after him some quizzing insinuation as to the nature of my message, which, coming from that quarter, and uttered in all the thoughtless levity of gaiety and dissipation, sounded sadly enough in my ear.

"Follow me," said Jennings, drily, and led the way to the parlour. Placing the candle on the chimneypiece, and standing close by the fireplace, he signed to me to shut the door, which I accordingly did; and when, in obedience to another sign, I had approached so near that our conversation could be distinctly carried on in tones little above a whisper, he continued, with manifest tokens of agitation—

"You came—you came from"—and abruptly stopped, looking at me with a pallid countenance, in which was stamped the intensest anxiety.

"I come, sir, with this note and a message," I replied, placing the letter in his hand.

He broke the seal and read the note hurriedly through, but without any change of expression; then looked at me with anxious abstraction for a second or two, and once more read the note through from end to end.

"And the—the patient," he added, fixing his eyes on me again; "you know—I suppose you know who she is?"

"Yes—Miss Chadleigh," I replied, with an effort.

"He knows it all," he muttered, scarce audibly, and looking at me still with the same abstracted and fear-stricken expression. "And how is she?" he asked after a pause—"is she safe?"

"She is doing well, sir," I replied; "she is safely over her trial."

"That's well," he said, drawing a long breath, as if relieved, but without exhibiting any corresponding cheer in the expression of his lace.

"And the infant," I began.

"Well," said he, quickly, "what of it?"

"Is also doing well," I replied—"a boy, the nurse desired me to tell you—a very fine boy, indeed."

"The nurse!" he repeated, while his face darkened with renewed alarm—"What nurse? Why, my great God! she's not mad enough—surely it can't—she's not at home?"

"No, indeed, sir, very far from her home, and not likely to be found either," I replied.

He seemed relieved; again took up the note, but replaced it on the table unread, and turned, and leaned his head on his hands on the chimney-piece, as it seemed, either buried in profound reflection, or wrung by some sudden agony. After a while he turned about, and thrusting his hands into his pockets, stood with his back to the fireplace, and his head sunk forward. The tight of the solitary candle upon the mantelpiece above him, deepened with its shadows the furrows of his contracted brow and down-drawn mouth. He looked, I thought, the very picture of comfortless and guilty wretchedness.

I had conceived instinctively, almost from the first moment I beheld him, a certain feeling of dislike toward Captain Jennings, and this predisposition my recent discoveries were, as you may readily suppose, by no means calculated to mitigate or remove. I could not help saying, in a tone which, had he been less agitated at the moment, might very possibly have provoked his anger—

"And may I ask, sir, have you no message of any kind for the unfortunate young lady?"

"Ay, ay, you're right; I forgot—to be sure," he answered, glancing quickly and anxiously around him; and then raising his hand in painful reflection to his face, replied— "You are very right—a message—yes, yes, yes."

As he said this, he mechanically took up the note again, and looking vacantly at it for a few seconds, threw it, as it seemed, unconsciously upon the table. My eyes followed it involuntarily, and as it fell before me (it is, I hope, needless to say, totally without my intending it, and merely in the accidental way in which the eye is often irresistibly fascinated by, and attracted to, exactly the object from which we are most anxious to avert it), I saw, and in some inappreciable fraction of a second, actually read the three first words of the note: they were—"Darling, darling husband." Turning it hastily face downward, I pushed it back again toward Captain Jennings.

"Husband!" unworthy as I believed the man to be, you would scarcely credit me were I to describe the sense of relief and delight with which my heart expanded as that one word met my eye. It seemed as if the voices of a thousand blessed angels were repeating it in melody and gratulations to my ear; in the glance that revealed it to me, I saw a creature rescued from the abyss of the darkest and most irretrievable of earthly ruin, and standing pure and safe in the light of heaven; my heart swelled within me, and tears rose to my eyes.

While those emotions agitated me, Captain Jennings continued lost in thought, and at last he said:—

"Ay, it is better to write;" and tearing off the outer leaf of the note which lay before him, he traced a line or two with his pencil, but checking himself, again paused, crumpled the note he had just commenced, and that he had received, together, applied them to the candle, and dropped them blazing into the grate.

"Say that I will be with her as soon as I can possibly get away," said he; "but where is the house—where is she?" he added, suddenly.

I described by the land-marks with which he was acquainted, exactly the spot where the poor young lady was to be found.

"Then, just say as I told you, that I will be there without one moment's avoidable delay."

Thus speaking, he hastily led the way to the hall-door; for some of his half-tipsy guests were beginning to call for him, and, as it seemed, were about making an exploratory excursion from the drawing-room. Muttering a broken curse upon them all, he opened the door, and I heard him, as I walked down the stone steps, respond in tones of affected gaiety to their clamorous challenge. With the rapid pace which indicates an excited mind, I retraced my steps; the bells were chiming, and the watchmen drowsily calling four o'clock, as I approached the scene of my strange adventure.

"Thank God, at all events," I fervently murmured— "thank God, the poor creature is not disgraced and ruined; a strange, perplexing, and, I fear, a most imprudent affair it unquestionably is; but, after all, what an escape!—how much to be thankful for!"

I had now reached my destination, and was admitted. The young lady, I was told, was doing well; so I delivered my message, and took my place in the parlour as before, resolved to await the departure of Doctor Robertson, who was still up stairs, and to explain, as was my fixed intention, the foolish accident which had involved me in the affair; acquaint him with my name and address, and assure him of my secresy.

I had not waited very long, when I heard him, with creaking steps, slowly descending the stairs, issuing, as he did, some parting directions to the woman who attended him with the candle.

"I shall look in the evening, after dark," he said; "everything promises fairly,—so that will do; I'll make my own way out; never mind—good morning."

As the worthy man uttered these gruff civilities, I presented myself at the foot of the stairs, and requested a word with him in the parlour. Merely directing me to be brief, and with a prodigious yawn, he accompanied me thither. I then proceeded to lay before him a full statement concerning myself, and the causes of my participation in the business. He was first disposed to be angry; but my own frankness and perhaps an old acquaintance with my father, an intimate of his youth, disarmed him, and my explanation ended by his shaking me good-naturedly by the hand.

"Egad, I believe I have been in greater fault of the two, young gentleman, in this affair," he said; "for I undertook my part with my eyes open; and a troublesome and an awkward part it must e'en prove, at the best. But," he added, in a changed tone, "with all its trouble and awkwardness, I would not have declined it for a thousand pounds; poor little thing; no, no; this was a matter of life or death; the poor child reposed confidence in me, and trusted me with the secret of her situation, under the seal of silence. I could not honourably divulge it; nor could I, with one particle of common humanity, refuse my aid; her life was in the balance; she would have had none attend her but me, and without proper assistance must have died; to have declined that aid, through any consideration of consequences affecting myself, would have been the act of a respectable scoundrel; it would have been to perpetrate a prudential murder."

As he spoke, there came a hurried knocking at the hall-door.

"This must be Captain Jennings," I said.

"Umph! he must not go up suddenly; they must prepare her for the meeting," said he; and, opening the chamber door, he said to the attendant—

"Shew Captain Jennings, if this be he, into this chamber; and as soon as you think the lady sufficiently recovered to see him, you can tell him so."

With this direction, he re-entered the room, and walked up and down once or twice, with rather an inauspicious expression of countenance, while he awaited the appearance of the new visitor; he had not long to wait; the door opened, and Captain Jennings, muffled in a cloak, entered the comfortless apartment.

Doctor Robertson received him with a stiff nod. After a few brief inquiries, rather drily answered, the physician said, in reply to a significant glance which Jennings had directed toward me—

"You need have no apprehension on account of his presence, Captain Jennings; whatever you have to say to me, may be said before him; he already knows all that is of moment in this affair, and his honour may be relied on."

"Honour!" repeated Jennings; "so then he's a gentleman, as I suspected."

"Permit me, Captain Jennings," said Doctor Robertson, "to recommend to you, what I conceive honour and common-sense alike indicate, as the proper course to be pursued in this painful affair. I have not had until this moment, it is true, an opportunity of so much as even speaking to you upon this subject, and do not know, even if I had, that I was at liberty to introduce it. I can have now, however, no scruple in fully telling you my mind; and I must say, that the extreme imprudence into which you have led an inexperienced and fondly-attached girl, threatens seriously to compromise her, not only with her own relatives, but in the eyes of the world. You have placed her in a situation calculated, unless it be at once explained, to prejudice her reputation fatally; and I am bound to say, as an old friend of the family, that unless you come forward frankly, and put Sir Arthur in possession of the real state of facts, I shall feel it my duty to do so myself."

"There is no need of any disclosure—at least immediately," said the young man, hurriedly. "Everything is arranged. No one but her old attendant has access to her chamber at home, and Sir Arthur and young Chadleigh don't see her once in five weeks. They don't suspect anything, and need not. Is it not clear that an explosion—a scene—just now, would be about the worst thing in the world for her?"

"Very true," said Doctor Robertson, drily; "all very true; but if there be an explosion, there is no need it should reach her ears. No, no, sir. Believe me, the only honourable course now open before you, is that of promptitude and candour. You ought, without the delay of an hour, to acquaint Sir Arthur with the fact of your marriage."

"And who the devil—" began Jennings, with a look which partook at once of rage and terror. The expression remained fixed for a time, but the sentence died away unfinished; and muttering some incoherent words, he walked, with a sort of half-agitated, half-defiant air, twice or thrice across the floor, and stopping at the empty fireplace, planted his foot upon the bar, and stood looking vacantly into the inhospitable grate, with an aspect as black and cheerless as its own.

"Well, sir," said Doctor Robertson, somewhat sternly, "you will, of course, act as you think proper; but I again advise you to be the first to open this affair to Sir Arthur; for, as I have already told you, he shall otherwise learn it all from myself. I have a very strong opinion about it."

"Of course, of course," said Jennings, petulantly; and continued, in a haughtier tone, perhaps intended to show Doctor Robertson that his further pursuing the subject would be considered impertinent—"By the way, sir, I ought to have thanked you before this for your able professional assistance."

"Sir, I intended no obligation whatever to you. My interest is naturally strongly engaged on the poor young lady's account," replied Doctor Robertson, gruffly, as he buttoned up his great-coat to his chin, and then drew on his warm gloves; "for her I would, if need were, do a great deal more."

He turned, stiffly and grimly, from the young man, shook me again by the hand, and took his departure.

Almost at the same moment, in obedience to an intimation from the attendant, Captain Jennings proceeded up the stairs, to the chamber where the young lady lay. As he followed the matron up stairs, the wailing of a new-born baby reached his ears. This feeble and plaintive appeal to his paternal sympathies, was probably far from welcome; for he looked as if, but for very shame, he would have cursed the helpless little creature; and now he stood at the chamber-door. Perhaps some touch of better feelings moved him, for his look grew sadder and softened. He entered. Faint, and with eyes half-closed, the fair young mother—her sore trial over—lay in the hushed and darkened room. Weak and exhausted as she was, a faint cry of joy broke from her pale lips; and such a look of ecstasy welcomed his appearance, as must have moved a heart of stone.

"Oh! Richard, Richard—oh! Richard," was all the poor creature could say, as he stooped over the bed and kissed her, with at least a show of fondness; while her feeble arm was clasped round his neck with an agony of delight, as if she had never hoped to have seen him again.

"Oh! Richard—Richard, darling!—it is you—darling, it is you!"

She clung to him, sobbing, and smiling, and softly repeating words of endearment, till, gently disengaging himself, he kissed her again, clasped her hand in his, and pressed it, and wrung it fondly, as he sat by the bedside. Thus silently testifying his affection, he leaned back, so that the curtain interposed between his face and hers. Two or three bitter tears started down his cheeks, and such a look of unutterable anguish darkened his countenance, as might have shadowed the eternal despair of the damned. Thus some minutes passed, while he pressed the feeble hand he held with a feverish grasp.

This interview was prolonged to more than an hour; and at length Jennings, warned by the approach of the dawn, took his departure, in sore disorder and dismay—his heart agitated with a tumult of terrible passions and sensations, his brain burning with a thousand wild and irreconcilable plans and projects—a thoroughly miserable man.

Meanwhile, I had returned to my lodgings, and thrown myself into bed, not to awaken to the remembrance of my last night's strange adventure until late in the day. It is, of course, unnecessary to say, that I felt the intensest curiosity respecting the progress and final denouement of this extraordinary affair. The conclusion was not long suspended.

Jennings had returned to his chamber in Kildare-street; but repose for him was out of the question. He had spent hours of agonized uncertainty; but at last his mind was made up, and his resolution taken.

"I have but one course to take—necessity controls me—I have no choice left" he muttered. "What infernal influence could have possessed me!—what accursed witchcraft can have blinded and infatuated me! Great God! what a serious, what a frightful business, it is turning out. Well, I suppose it was my destiny. I wonder if that old fellow had any inkling of my real situation when he forbid me his house? Merciful Heaven! if I had but acted then like a man of common sense; but some accursed delusion was over me. I had got interested and piqued in the pursuit. I did not dream of mischief. I could swear, with my dying breath, I never meant harm, until accident and the devil—and poor, poor Mary herself—put that accursed piece of madness into my head. Curse my folly! It is a desperate, a frightful situation; but self-preservation is, they say, the first law of nature; and were I even to sacrifice myself, I don't see that she would be essentially the better." He consulted his watch, and continued—"My measures must be taken promptly; that meddling, doctorfellow, will be on the fidgets till he does mischief. I can't be too prompt."

He rang the bell, directed the servant peremptorily to deny him to all visitors, drew the window-blinds, bolted the door, and then, seating himself before his desk, wrote, with painful attention and assiduity, for full two hours, without rising. This task completed, he carefully raised the manuscript, making various erasures and interpolations, and at last, folded carefully, sealed it, and placing it in his waistcoat pocket (in those days a tolerably capacious receptacle), he buttoned his coat across it.

"Will he do it?" he muttered, doubtfully; "we'll see—we'll see. In the first place, he may never be called on to say a word, pro or con; in the second, even if he be, this is as easily said as anything else; and, in the third, we will gild the pill pretty thickly."

So saying, he opened a drawer in the desk, and took out a handful of guineas and a bundle of bank notes, the spoils of his last night's successful play.

"Let me see what have I got in bank," he reflected; "I must leave enough for my part of the business; it would not do to be money-bound just now. Ay, ay, he may have the three hundred. I think three hundred will be strong enough for him. Poor Mary—poor Mary!"

Having counted out, in notes and guineas, the sum he had named, he rolled them up, and stuffed them into his pocket; then muffling his face in a shawl, and putting on his hat and cloak, he sallied forth upon an expedition, of the last importance to his plans.

✺

It was drawing towards evening, upon the same day, when a servant called at my lodgings with a note, and sent up word that he waited for an answer. I did not know the hand, but expecting an invitation, nevertheless, I broke

the seal eagerly, and read the following—to a very different purport, as you may perceive:—

"Kildare-street

"Captain Jennings presents his compliments
to Mr. ——, and trusts that he will pardon the
liberty which, under very peculiar circumstances,
he takes, in venturing to entreat the favour of his
(Mr. ——'s) presence for a few moments, upon a
matter of the utmost importance, as respects an
affair in which he has already evinced an interest. Captain Jennings has an engagement for this
evening, but will be at home till seven o'clock;
and will esteem it a real obligation if Mr. ——
will honour him with a call at any time before
that hour."

I instantly wrote a civil answer, complying with his request; and, full of impatience for the result, I prepared to
follow the messenger without losing a moment.

My preparations were quickly made, and I was soon
in the street, and traversing the intervening space between mine and Captain Jennings' lodgings at a rapid
pace. As I turned the corner of Nassau-street, I met my
friend ——, a notorious gossip in his day. I perceived,
by his at once taking my arm, and turning about with
me, that he had a story to tell, and was rather shocked at
his opening sentence—

"Well, what do you think of the affair in Stephen's-
green?—of course you have heard it all—about the
Chadleighs; a shocking piece of business, upon my life—a
devilish fine girl, too—a great pity."

I affected surprise, and asked the particulars.

"Somewhere about twelve o'clock to-day," he said, "old Sir Arthur received an invitation—at least so I'm told, for I have not yet had time to sift the matter myself—an invitation for himself and Miss Chadleigh, they say, to old Lady ——'s down in what-d'ye-call-it—that place in Kildare, you know; and they say—egad, I can scarce help laughing, though I'm devilish sorry too—they tell me her ladyship mentioned, by way of inducement, that young Lord Dungarret, an admirer, as it was thought, of Miss Chadleigh, was to be there; and this consideration determined the old boy to accept it, come what might, though his daughter had been ailing for a long time. And so he took his crutches, and hobbled up to her room, where he had not been for a month before, to tell her—ha! ha!—his sovereign will and pleasure; but, egad, the old boy had his hobble for nothing, for, rat me, the bird was flown, the cage was empty; the invalid had absconded, the fair lady had fled; how, why, whither, or with whom, remains a profound secret."

"And when did she go?" I asked, anxious to ascertain how far the particulars were known.

"Oh, last night, and it is supposed by the back way," he replied; "it was devilish well managed—a clever girl, sir—a deep scheme."

"Do they suspect the purpose or the companion of her flight?" I inquired.

"The purpose!—poh, poh! that's plain enough; I have not heard yet who was the gallant gay—but I forgot to tell you, by-the-bye, the old fellow—old Sir Arthur—put himself into such a devil of a frenzy, when he found it out, that he got a sort of a fit—a devilish bad fit, I am told. Poor old fellow! he is a deuced deal too purple and bull-necked to stand excitement. I should not be a bit surprised if he's done for—regularly done for. There goes Dr. Robertson's carriage—egad, direct to Stephen's-green, too; I venture an even guinea, he's going straight to shave and blister old Chadleigh. You know he's their family physician—a great oddity, a perfect character. I'm told Lady Chadleigh, poor woman! used to say, whenever—by the way, it's odd how things run in the blood—there's Miss Chadleigh just taking after her mother, a run-away already."

Here he broke off, for, seeing a friend at the other side of the street, he hastened across to tell the news to a fresh listener, and leaving me opportunity enough, for we had just reached the corner of Kildare-street, and for many reasons, I had no wish that he should see me enter Jennings' lodgings.

What I had just heard, satisfied me that the catastrophe, whatever it might be, was certainly not far distant; and with a degree of anxiety proportioned to the imminence of the event, in which I could not help feeling the profoundest interest, I knocked at the hall-door, and was promptly shewn up stairs, and found myself vis-a-vis with Captain Jennings.

I found him in his dressing-gown and slippers. He looked pale and anxious, but had quite recovered his coolness and self-possession by this time.

"I feel that I have taken a great liberty, in giving you so much trouble," he continued, after the usual salutations had been interchanged, and I had taken a chair; "but, with the exception of Doctor Robertson, with whom my acquaintance is just as slight as with you, I have no other gentleman to apply to in this most unhappy affair"—(here he slightly shrugged his shoulders, with an air of chagrin and discontent, which somehow impressed me more than all that had yet passed, with a conviction of that callous selfishness which I believed to be the basis of his character)—"You and Doctor Robertson are alone acquainted with the particulars of this business, and you will, I trust, forgive the preference which makes me, not, perhaps, unnaturally, select you, rather than him, as the depository of the only confidence I have to make."

He said this in his most engaging and conciliatory manner; but, as I bowed in acknowledgment of the preference, I felt my original dislike of him rather increased than abated.

"I offer no defence whatever for my conduct; God knows I blame myself as severely as anybody else can possibly do," he continued, with a contrite shake of the head; "I ran blindly into extreme temptation, and have compromised, not only myself, but a young lady, whom I would gladly die to extricate from the unfortunate position into which I have unguardedly led her."

Equivocal as had been his agitation that morning, it was, at all events, genuine; but now he had recalled all the artificial graces of his manner. I saw in the polished ease of his remorse, and in the studied melancholy of his compassion, something indescribably repulsive and abominable.

"Without further tasking your patience," he resumed, at the same time taking a paper from his desk, "I have to entreat your consent to become the depository of this paper. It is a piece of evidence which may throw an important light upon this affair; the copy of a document, which I keep in my possession, and which you will, perhaps, oblige me by retaining in yours; the nature of it you will see at a glance, and I have endorsed upon it the name and address of the party whose testimony it is, so that, if need be, there can be no difficulty in applying it properly. All I ask of you is, to guard it equally from destruction, and from the eyes of all others, but yourself; and that, whenever I write to you to that effect, you will kindly hand it to my law-agent in town, whom I will name to you, whenever it becomes necessary to employ one. Will you kindly undertake this commission?"

I could hardly decline an office, as it seemed, so easily performed. I so little liked the applicant himself, however, that a slight, and not very gracious hesitation, preceded my acceptance of its duties. He thanked me, however, profusely; and I had risen for the purpose of taking my departure, when a vehicle of some kind stopped at the hall-door, and a thundering double-knock announced the arrival of a visitor.

"Tell them I'm dressing," said Jennings to the servant, who appeared at the room-door; and, in the next moment, the summons at the hall-door was answered.

"Captain Jennings is dressing for the evening," I heard the servant say, in reply to the inquiry of the footman who had knocked.

This intimation, however, had not the desired effect, for the steps of the carriage were let down with a sharp clang, and, almost at the same moment, I heard a different voice, that, I presumed, of the visitor in person, demand—

"Is your master at home?"

The same answer was repeated, and the applicant for admission replied in a sharp decisive tone—

"Ha! dressing for the evening, very good; then he is at home?"

"But, sir, I beg pardon; he positively cannot see anybody at present," urged the man.

"He shall certainly see me," retorted the visitor, in the same tone. "I know the way—don't mind."

From the moment the clatter of the carriage-steps smote my ear, my mind unaccountably misgave me, and a foreboding of impending collision and mischief, filled me with an almost painful suspense. My instinctive apprehensions did not deceive me. The drawing-room door was pushed abruptly open, and young Chadleigh entered the room.

The moment I saw him, I perceived that in his face which warned me of the truth of my vague anticipations. Pale, stern, and collected, he walked slowly a few steps into the room, bowed with an ominous and icy formality to Captain Jennings, and, in a tone so cold and deadly, as I think I never heard before, or since, said—

"Captain Jennings, I presume you apprehend the subject of my visit?"

It was scarcely necessary to put the question. He had advanced to receive Chadleigh with his usual air of frank and easy gaiety, their eyes met, and in the encounter he read the truth—the smile passed away in an instant from his countenance, and was succeeded by a look, to the full as stern and ominous as that which confronted him. The young men felt that a deadly quarrel lay between them, and I think I never saw a more portentous greeting.

"You have not announced it, sir," said Jennings, with cold and measured politeness; "but I have no hesitation in saying, that I do suspect the cause of your visit."

"Good, sir!" replied Chadleigh, in the same constrained voice; "I came on behalf of Miss Mary Chadleigh's father, and in my own right, as her brother, to demand of you, in the first place, where that young lady at present is."

"Without meaning to dispute your right to put that question," replied Jennings, "I mean to stand upon mine, to decline answering it."

"You refuse to answer?" said his visitor, while his countenance darkened.

"I do—most distinctly refuse," repeated he.

"Pray, think better of it, sir," retorted Chadleigh, with a ghastly mimicry of courtesy.

"Mr. Chadleigh," replied Jennings, haughtily, "I recommend you strongly to act as a man of the world in this business. The mischief, whatever it be, is now post cure. If you will only allow events to take their course, scandal may be avoided, and a great deal of unnecessary trouble, exposure, and violence spared. If you will persist in pushing this matter to extremity, do so; upon your head be the consequences."

"Sir," said Chadleigh, "you greatly mistake me, if you fancy that your mean and perfidious conduct, in spiriting away the daughter of a gentleman, who frankly told you that he peremptorily declined the connexion which your conduct seemed to offer—if you fancy that your base and mercenary conduct in inveigling her, a young lady entitled to a fortune, and with most suitable prospects before her, into a marriage with you, a mere adventurer—"

"Mr. Chadleigh, before you proceed further, let me ask you, have you actually made up your mind to push this affair to a public quarrel?" insisted Jennings.

"Yes, sir," retorted Chadleigh, proudly and bitterly. "Mary Chadleigh has selected for herself—embraced her own degradation—married a man whom her father expressly forbid his house, because he suspected him of entertaining the schemes he has but too securely realized. She is now, and henceforward, to Sir Arthur and to me, a stranger; we renounce and disown her; and by ——, she shall not stand between you and the punishment you deserve." He paused; and added emphatically—"I presume you will be at home by eleven o'clock tonight?"

"Certainly, sir," answered Jennings, calmly.

His visitor bowed sternly, and began to withdraw.

"I wish, if you please, to add one word," said Jennings.

"Certainly," said Chadleigh, returning.

Jennings looked down for a moment, in agitated and guilty abstraction—bit his lips, and grew deadly pale, as though inwardly agonized with a mortal struggle.

"I have to request your attention, too, Mr. ——" he said, addressing me, and arresting my departure. "It is, unfortunately, due to myself that you should hear what I am about to say."

"Be so good as to say, without further delay, what you desire me to hear," said Chadleigh.

"Yes, sir; you have forced me to it," said Jennings, drawing himself up, and looking with a steady, and singularly evil scowl, full in his visitor's face. "You talked of marriage?"

"Yes, sir," replied Chadleigh.

"Well, sir, as you will have it a quarrel between us, it is, unfortunately, due to myself to say, that there is no such thing as marriage in the case."

Jennings spoke these words with a resolute and measured distinctness which left no room for misapprehension.

"No!—no marriage!" said Chadleigh, after a hideous pause of some seconds, and speaking almost in a whisper, like one half-stunned, while he returned the guilty gaze of his transformed friend with a stare of actual horror.

For my own part, I confess I was scarcely one degree less astounded than Chadleigh, at this utterly unlooked for declaration.

"Not married—not married! Why, great God, can it— is it credible! You monstrous, measureless villain—"

The flimsy varnish of affected courtesy was gone, and the hell-born passions it had masked broke forth in an instant, in undisguised and titanic revelation. With one hoarse execration, shrieked rather than spoken, Chadleigh advanced toward Jennings.

"Take care, Chadleigh—take care; I would not harm you," said Jennings, sternly.

"Hold, for God's sake," I cried, interposing between the two young men. "Mr. Chadleigh, I implore of you—remember, consider; what can come of this?"

"Let me go, sir," cried Chadleigh, hoarsely.

"Mr. Jennings," I cried, still clinging to Chadleigh, for in his furious paroxysm of excitement, I could not tell what dreadful results might possibly attend a physical encounter, "for God's sake, avoid this; you'll have bloodshed else. Mr. Chadleigh, reflect; stay for one moment."

"Let me go, sir; let me go, or by ——, I'll strike you down," cried Chadleigh, straining and struggling to reach the object of his fury.

"Get into your room, Mr. Jennings, unless you wish for murder. Go, for Heaven's sake," I repeated. "I can't prevent it longer. I tell you go—go, in God's name. Will you go, or not?"

Jennings' momentary agitation had entirely disappeared with the immediate menace of such an encounter as that which threatened him. His physical courage no one had ever doubted; and the moment it was tasked, his intrepid calmness instantly returned. He hesitated for a second; then, with one glance of mingled remorse and disdain at Chadleigh. He turned, and strode sullenly into his chamber, flinging the door close after him. The key was, fortunately, in the outside; and, without giving Chadleigh time to get before me, I sprang to the door, locked it, and, placing the key in my pocket, stood facing the baffled assailant.

"Sir," he said bitterly, "by ——, you shall answer for this."

"When and how you please, Mr. Chadleigh," I replied, sadly. "I have done my duty, and no more, in preventing a murderous fray; and I thank God I have succeeded."

He stood undecided for a few seconds. At last he said—

"Perhaps you were right, sir; and I ought to ask your pardon. You were right, sir, and I was wrong. Pardon me."

I gave him the assurance he required, and he added abruptly—

"This is no place for me. Good night, sir."

So saying, he left the room; and I, from the window, saw him re-enter the carriage, and drive away, ere I returned to turn the key in Jennings' room. I did so, and called him; there was no answer. I pushed the door open a little, and looked in. He had thrown himself into a chair, and was sitting close by a table, his forehead laid upon his arm, and his face concealed—he was sobbing. He started up abruptly, on becoming aware of my presence, and with a violent effort commanded himself.

"Mr. ——," said he, "pray don't leave me, for a few minutes. Mr. ——, you don't know what I am suffering, and what I have suffered. I am about the most miserable and unfortunate mortal you have ever seen or heard of—indeed I am. Sir, you can't understand—I can't explain to you the horrors of my position."

"The poor young lady," I said, coldly, "is certainly impressed with the belief that she is legally married. Dr. Robertson distinctly told me so—nay, he himself believed it."

"Yes, yes, yes," he interrupted, vehemently; "but I can prove it is not so. The paper I have placed in your hand will show you that there has been no such thing. She thinks it—she believes, no doubt, poor creature; but she's wrong—quite wrong."

I was greatly shocked at the sinister eagerness with which Jennings laboured to impress this fact, which, of all others I thought he ought naturally to be most anxious to conceal for the present, upon my conviction; and I could not forbear saying—

"At all events, you will not fail to make all the reparation now in your power, and—"

"What reparation?" he asked, vehemently.

"There is but one," I answered, "which you can now offer; and that is, marriage."

"You are right, indeed," he answered, sullenly, after a long pause; "it is the only—the only reparation for such a wrong."

He sank into a moody and compunctious silence. At last he said, abruptly—

"They talk of generosity, and impulse, and all that, but take my word for it, prudence is worth them all. My own utter want of reflection has done it. I have been drawn into a situation in which I am powerless, at least for good; but do me justice, sir; you must do me justice, for, by ———, I designed no wrong; I am not a cold-blooded wretch. I was led away by passion—misguided and betrayed into a position, as I told you, where I am no longer a free agent, and then my conduct is criticised, as if I could do just as I pleased. Is this justice or honesty? I'm railed at like a cold, scheming villain, and damned for not making reparation—I, that never laid a deliberate plot in my life, or hesitated to make atonement where I could. By heavens, sir, I tell you truth. Is this fair dealing—is it candour—is it common toleration?"

I reminded Jennings that I had no right to judge in the matter; and also intimated that I had already staid too long, and so rose to take my departure.

"Well, well, well," he said, with a dreary sort of shrug; "patience, and shuffle the cards—who knows what may turn up—who knows? Though, egad, take it which way you will, it is about as cursed, black a looking business, as ever man was in for. It is hard—hard, by ———. It looks as if they were all in a savage conspiracy to ruin me; and what good, in the devil's name, can come of it—a pack of fools!"

I now took my leave. A feeling of curiosity, and, still more strongly, one of intense interest in the unfortunate young lady, with whose fate he was so disastrously connected, had tempted me, minute after minute, to prolong my visit. It was already nearly dark, and the street-lamps were burning. I had reached the corner of Grafton-street, buried in profound abstraction, when I was suddenly accosted by a familiar voice. It was that of my friend Fitzgerald, a wild fellow, and a pleasant one to boot, and an accomplished adept in all the then important mysteries of the small-sword and pistol, and learned in all the lore of points of honour.

"Can you tell me," said he, after our greeting, and taking me at the same time by the arm, and drawing me with him, "whether Dick Chadleigh has got into a scrape?"

"What kind of a scrape do you mean?" I asked, evasively.

"Why, he called on me when I was out, not half-an-hour ago," he replied, "and left a hurried note, telling me I must go to him without a moment's delay, on my return, about a little business. Now, there is but one kind of business I understand"—here he raised his arm once or twice significantly, as if balancing a pistol—"and I strongly suspect it must be upon that he has called me to counsel; all my friends make use of me, you know, on such occasions. Have you heard anything of Chadleigh's being likely to want my services in that way—eh?"

I told him I knew that high words had passed between him and Captain Jennings.

"Jennings—ho, ho!" said he, with a serious air—"a cool hand, I fancy. Egad, from the little I've seen of him, I'm inclined to think, if he is the man, it will be a matter of flints and powder—egad, it does look like business."

I was not at all sorry to comply with Fitzgerald's suggestion, to the effect that I should await his return in Brown's coffee-house, and end the evening there in his company. My anxiety to learn the issue of the business was such, that I would gladly have done much more to satisfy it. Accordingly, I dropt into that public resort of idleness, while Fitzgerald, having called a coach, rumbled away to his interview with Chadleigh.

I had sat there for considerably more than an hour, and was beginning to give up all hope of his return, when he entered.

"Well," said he, when we had established ourselves at a table apart from the rest, "I have had a couple of odd—devilish odd conversations—since I saw you. I don't know, indeed, whether I am at liberty to tell you the subject of the quarrel."

I interrupted him by assuring him that I already knew it; and having satisfied him upon this point, he proceeded to detail the particulars, which I shall condense for the benefit of the reader.

He had, it seemed, found Chadleigh still much excited, and quite determined upon a hostile meeting; indeed, so resolute upon the point, that he would not so much as hear of anything to the contrary. His directions were peremptory, and amounted simply to this—that arrangements for a meeting were to be completed without a moment's delay. All details, of course, were left to the direction of his friend; with respect to the quarrel itself, however, he was not invested with any right of diplomacy. Finding Chadleigh thus implacably resolved, Fitzgerald undertook the affair, which for other parties he had so often filled with singular efficiency, and was duly invested with the important functions of a "second" in the affair. Leaving Chadleigh, however, and being still of opinion that, if possible, the matter ought, for every reason, to be quietly adjusted, he resolved, upon his own responsibility, to make one final effort to prevent a catastrophe which, even if unattended by any more tragical consequences, must, at all events, have the effect of irreparably disgracing Miss Chadleigh. His belief was, that there remained one chance, and one only, of saving the unfortunate young lady and that was, a private marriage with the author of her shame, accomplished without the delay of a single hour, if possible, so that the public might hear of the elopement and the marriage at one and the same time. Filled with this project, Fitzgerald hurried up the stairs of Jennings' lodgings. The servant announced him as he entered the drawing-room. Jennings had altered his purpose, and determined, after what had passed, to remain at home. He was still in his dressing-gown, and, when his visitor entered, was sitting before his open desk, the candles burning beside him, and what seemed like a miniature in his hands. He was looking intently upon it, with no very loving aspect, when Fitzgerald entered; but he hastily thrust it, face downward, among the open letters, which lay in multitudinous confusion in the profundity of the old-fashioned desk, and shutting all up quickly, he locked it fast, and rose to receive him. Fitzgerald observed, also, that some torn papers were burning on the fire, and Jennings glanced quickly towards them, to see that they were actually destroyed.

"I have the honour, Captain Jennings, to wait upon you with a communication from Mr. Chadleigh," said Fitzgerald.

"Pray, sir, take a chair," said Jennings, coldly, and with a formal bow.

Fitzgerald complied, and resumed—

"I need scarcely, I apprehend, detail the reasons which have induced this step. You have already had an interview with my principal, Mr. Chadleigh."

"There is certainly no occasion, sir, to say more. I do perfectly understand the nature of your visit, which I have, indeed, been expecting; and have only to say, as Mr. Chadleigh has pushed matters to extremity, I apprehend your instructions are very brief, and that our present business may be quickly arranged; if you will favour me with your card, my friend shall wait upon you at whatever hour you name."

"To say the truth, Mr. Jennings," replied Fitzgerald, "you are right in supposing that my instructions have been very brief—in a word, they were those of absolute and unconditional hostility; this, however, is a case of such very peculiar delicacy—a case in which forbearance is so eminently important—so imperatively called for by all the circumstances, that I have resolved to take a responsibility upon myself, and endeavour to arrange this matter amicably, if, indeed, it be possible."

Jennings continued to regard him with earnest attention, but did not speak.

"In short, as far as my influence goes, I would guarantee such an adjustment, upon one condition, which you can have no possible objection in submitting to—that you repair the dishonour you have done Miss Chadleigh, by marrying her, before her present unhappy position becomes public."

Jennings grew deadly pale, and his features seemed to contract with the intensity of acute suffering, as he gazed for a few seconds upon the speaker, and then, abruptly rising, with a gesture like wringing his hands he turned towards the fire, and remained standing for a time with his face averted.

"Well, sir," exclaimed Fitzgerald, after a pause of considerable surprise—for he had expected a prompt and grateful acceptance of his proffered interposition—"what do you say—what am I to understand?"

Jennings heaved a dreary sigh, and said, gloomily and desperately enough—

"What you propose is absolutely out of the question—impracticable."

"Then, sir, take the consequences," said Fitzgerald, with irrepressible indignation; "you have, at least, quieted my scruples in acting against you—there is but one way of settling the matter now."

"Just so, sir," said Jennings, who had recovered his haughty coldness; "and, as I must leave details to the discretion of my friend, I have only to ask you at what hour precisely it will be convenient to you to see him?"

Fitzgerald named ten o'clock that night, and placed his card in Jennings' hand.

"Very good, sir," replied the latter, having glanced at it; "I presume that both parties are equally anxious to have this affair concluded with all possible despatch; my friend shall attend at the appointed hour."

With these words they parted.

"I don't know how it is," said Fitzgerald, after he had concluded his narrative, "but this thing has put me quite out of spirits—it is a bad affair, a d—d bad business; and, mark my words, so sure as you sit there, one or other of them will lose his life by it; they are both of them game—game to the back-bone—game every inch, sir; and Chadleigh is in a murderous, black temper, too. Somehow, this is the first business of the sort, I ever had a hand in, that made me mopish; d—n me, but it smells all over of death and winding-sheets."

As the mortal crisis of this strange tragedy approached, my interest in its denouement became more and more intense. At my entreaty, Fitzgerald undertook to let me know, so soon as they were completed, the detailed arrangements for the approaching duel. As he had sundry preparations to make, he was obliged to leave me, and I walked home, in dejected solitude, to my lodgings.

I was no sooner alone in my apartment, than I recollected the paper which had been entrusted to my care by

Jennings. He had not only omitted to prohibit its perusal in my case, but had actually told me, in so many words, that I was at liberty to read it. There was, therefore, no impediment to the honourable gratification of my curiosity; and, secure from interruption, I proceeded to examine the document.

It purported to be a statement of certain occurrences, in connexion with a clandestine visit made by the deponent, one "Benjamin Cruise, clerk, resident next door to the Cow and Cleaver, in Smithfield, in the city of Dublin;" at the solicitation of Mrs. Martha Keating, at the house of Sir Arthur Chadleigh, in St. Stephen's-green. The narrative was to the effect, that the reverend gentleman in question was applied to, on or about a certain day, nearly a year preceding the date of the document in question, to attend at the back entrance of the said mansion; where, according to arrangement, he waited until about one o'clock, when he was admitted, and conveyed with great precaution up a back-stair, and into a chamber, where was a young lady, as it seemed, in much agitation; and whom, as he was then and there informed by the old woman, his conductress, he believes to have been Miss Mary Chadleigh; by which name, he was afterwards directed to marry her to a certain young gentleman, whom he now knows to be Captain Jennings, and who, shortly after his, Cruise's arrival, joined the party in the said chamber, with like caution; that he, Cruise, had then, at the desire of the party, proceeded to unite Miss Chadleigh and Captain Jennings, according to the ritual of the Church of England; and that a noise in another part of the house having alarmed them, the ceremony was interrupted in the introductory part, and before the giving of the ring; and he and Captain Jennings, were together hurried out from the house the same way; and, that he never before, or since then, saw Miss

Mary Chadleigh, and knew not of her having been married by any other clergyman. This statement, which was given with great aggravation of detail, was duly dated, and signed in full, by the reverend gentleman, in those days, a not very creditably-notorious personage.

The perusal of this document impressed me still more unfavourably respecting Jennings. There was something sinister and equivocal about the whole thing. The infamous character of the degraded man who signed it; the industrious detail with which it had been prepared; and, above all, the unaccountable precaution which had suggested the adoption of such a measure, filled me with painful misgivings, to the effect that some gross and horrible delusion had been practised upon poor Miss Chadleigh; and I could not forbear deeply regretting, that I had suffered myself, under conditions of secrecy, to be made the depository of so suspicious a document.

I was pursuing this unsatisfactory train of reflections when a note was placed in my hand; it was couched in the following terms:—

"Dear ——,
At seven o'clock to-morrow morning, on the Fifteen Acres.

"Yours in haste,
"Fitzgerald."

I spent a restless night, and was up long before dawn. Having completed my toilet, I walked some way into town, in the grey twilight of coming morning; and when I had, as I calculated, consumed the greater part of the necessary interval, I got into a hackney-coach, and drove directly to the place of rendezvous. Availing myself of a screen of bushes, I stopped the carriage, and got out, unobserved from the scene of action. As soon as I obtained a view of the ground, I observed there a coach, and a little group of three persons, who were standing, listlessly, close beside it; two or three gentlemen on horseback—mere spectators, of course, like myself—were also on the ground. I walked as near as I decently could to the group I have mentioned, and saw that Chadleigh and Fitzgerald were two of the number. The latter looked at his watch, and mounted the coachbox, to command a more extended view; shading his eyes with his hand, he looked along the skirting of wood which bounds the place, in the direction of the city, and at last his eye seemed to settle upon a distant object. I followed the direction of his gaze, and saw the top of a carriage moving in the distance.

"Here," I thought, "comes Jennings; which of them is to leave the field unhurt, and which—" I shrank from the inquiry, merely mental as it was, with something like a shudder.

"Poor Mary Chadleigh! whichever way it ends, its issue must be, to her, a tragedy."

Fitzgerald had descended from his post of observation, and recognizing me, he walked up, and shook me by the hand. He looked pale and stern.

"They are coming," said he, glancing towards the vehicle which was now rapidly approaching.

"Rather late—are they?" I asked—more from want of something to say than any other cause.

"No, no; a quarter past seven was fixed on, subsequently to my note, last night; we should scarcely have had light earlier," he said.

"The weapons are pistols?" I asked.

"Yes," he answered; "and we may as well begin to make our preparations. Come with me; you'll not be in the way; I won't stand on ceremony when the time comes for you to withdraw and leave Major Gurney and myself to our deliberations."

So saying, he drew me with him to the side of the carriage.

"Take out the case," he said to the man who stood by the carriage-door; "not that—those are the instruments; leave it where Dr. —— placed it—the flat case—that's right; just keep it in your hand; and when I beckon to you, bring it over to me quickly; there, don't shake it."

We now walked up to Chadleigh, who stood moodily and doggedly, with his surtout buttoned up to the chin; and exchanging, now and then, a brief word or two with his companion—a slim, pale-faced, young surgeon, who was, evidently, but one degree less frightened than if he had been himself a principal. Fitzgerald dropped my arm as he approached, and leaving me at a little distance, observed, consulting his watch—

"Eight minutes before their time."

Chadleigh nodded.

"They have brought advice, too," suggested the little surgeon, timidly; "there is a second carriage."

"There's no need to waste time," said Chadleigh; "we had better walk on a little to meet them."

The steps of the first carriage had, by this time, been let down; and Jennings, followed by a stiff, elderly gentleman, with a red, important face, and a military air, descended upon the turf. After, as it seemed, a few directions to the servants, they began to walk towards us, briskly, followed by an attendant, carrying a pistol-case; and with the carriage, which carried their medical friend, a little in the rear.

My heart swelled within me as those two little groups approached one another, in grim silence, over the smooth sward. Gracious God! what an awful account for eternity was to be closed ere they parted!

On they came, briskly and steadily, through the keen and misty morning air—nearer and nearer—until the interposing space became so limited that each party, as it were, by mutual consent, slackening their pace, came slowly to a halt, at some dozen steps apart, and interchanged, in silence, a stern and formal salutation. Fitzgerald stept forward, and was met about half-way by the grim elderly gentleman whom I have described. After another salutation, as formal, they withdrew a little, and conducted a brief conference, in short, decisive whispers. Meanwhile, those who, either accidentally, or by design, had been spectators of the proceedings, began to gather about the spot on which the combatants were placed.

I had thought, once or twice, that Jennings perceived my presence, and now I was assured of it.

"Mr. ———," he said, in a low, hurried tone, "I have a request to make."

"Pray, state it, sir," I replied, approaching.

"It is just this—should I happen to fall, remain here for a few moments, as I may feel it necessary to make a communication to you of the last importance, not to myself, but to others."

I undertook to comply with this request, and withdrew.

There was not the slightest perceptible tremor, not the least indication of excitement, in his manner, voice, or aspect, excepting that he was, perhaps, a little paler than usual, and his eyes were unusually dilated. With the restlessness of suspense, I walked to the spot where Chadleigh was standing, and, almost at the same moment, Fitzgerald returned.

"What is the distance?" asked Chadleigh.

"Ten paces," rejoined Fitzgerald.

"Too much," said he, gruffly.

"It is the usual thing; you don't want to have us look blood-thirsty." retorted Fitzgerald.

"And for that reason, I'd like to have it settled one way or other at the first shot."

"It will be settled time enough," said the second, and, unlocking the pistol-case, he proceeded to load the weapons; a silence, hardly broken by a whisper, followed, during which the click of ramrods, and the cramming home of wadded bullets were ominously audible.

"Are you ready, Mr. Fitzgerald?" inquired Jennings' second; "if so, we had better place our men at once."

A piece of money was thrown up for choice of ground; Jennings won.

"Luck's so far with us, sir; I hope it may not turn," remarked the veteran, with a ghastly jocularity.

Chadleigh disencumbered himself of his surtout, and the combatants took their ground respectively.

"Gentlemen," said the major, addressing the spectators, "have the goodness to draw back a little; some of you may be hurt, else."

The suggestion was complied with, and a breathless silence followed.

"Are you ready, gentlemen," inquired the major.

Each answered in the affirmative.

After a brief pause the word "fire" was given, each raised his weapon, but Chadleigh only fired. Jennings must have had a narrow escape, for he shook his head, put his hand to his ear, as if a hornet had stung him, then, quickly raising the pistol, he fired into the air, threw the weapon up, and caught it by the muzzle as it descended.

"D—e, sir, that won't do," exclaimed Chadleigh, in a tone of bitter exasperation, "you may throw away your shot, if you will, but I'm cursed if you get out of the business on these terms; it is the act of a poltroon and a scoundrel to sneak out of a quarrel that way; I'll baulk your scheme, for you—"

"Don't say a word," said Jennings, sternly, interrupting Fitzgerald, who was about to interfere, "I call you all to witness I have stood his fire, and without returning it—that's all; let him take the consequences of his vindictive obstinacy. I'll not stand to be shot at like a target; I've a right to defend myself, and by —— I'll do it."

"Certainly; 'tis very just and sensible; the very point I was going to put," said the major, with a brisk approval, that strongly contrasted with the savage intensity of Jennings' tone.

It was plain that the angry and mortal passions of combat were, in Jennings, at last thoroughly aroused.

I heard him say to Major Gurney, once or twice, impatiently, "make haste," and saw him dart one or two lowering glances at Chadleigh. The preliminaries for a second exchange of shots were completed in a few moments—the signal was given—and both fired so exactly together, that, from the report, one would have believed the explosion a single one. Jennings' shot was well directed, though accident defeated its aim; it struck the trigger-guard of Chadleigh's pistol, which was nearly forced from his hand by the shock, and glancing off, the ball buried itself in the sod. Jennings, on the other hand, stood immovable, while one might slowly count three, then staggered a little, dropped his pistol, and fell suddenly to the ground. Chadleigh walked forward a few hesitating steps, checked himself, and, in an agitated voice, said to the surgeon who had accompanied him—

"You may be wanted here—by —— he's a hurt! Fitzgerald, come away—come, I say."

Meanwhile, amid a babel of conflicting and exciting suggestions, the surgeon, ordering the crowd to stand back, had the wounded man raised a little on the carriage cushions, and was proceeding to examine the injury, but Jennings said, faintly—

"Don't—don't—it's all of no use."

He invited me, with a glance and a slight gesture, to approach.

"One word," he said, speaking with great difficulty. I stooped down, to bring my ear as near him as I could. "It's all a lie—all that—the paper—see the man, and tell him I said so—poor Mary—I made him do it, but I could not help it—there's no use in maintaining the cheat any longer—I'm dying. Keep him away," he continued, faintly turning his gaze for a moment on the surgeon, who was approaching, and then on me, "he can do nothing for me—only listen to me—my last word—that paper is—is a lie—we were married—I can—I can scarcely speak— don't—don't—are you going—hold me—oh God!"

I can never forget the look that Jennings fixed on me— the fearful, imploring gaze of his dilated eyes, filled with the wild, deep, awful meaning of death—the strangling effort to speak—the ghastly pallor—and then, the drop- ping of the jaw—the mouth, through which the breath of life was never more to stir, helplessly agape—the eyes, with the deep earnestness of their awful meaning, fixed for ever—and the stern movelessness of the darkened brow. Was this the gay, vain, reckless Jennings? Was this mute but fearful monitor of death, propped-up before us, indeed the frivolous, light-hearted, sensual man of the world, among whose dreams and calculations the warning shadow of death had never glided?

"By —— he is dead," said one of the by-standers, breaking the breathless silence that had followed.

The surgeon kneeled down beside him, placed his hand over the dead man's heart, raised his arm, and held his pulse for a moment—then replaced the hand by his side in silence. I remember seeing the grass that he had plucked, dropping from the stiffening fingers.

"Lift the body into the carriage, and drive to Kildare-street," said the physician, addressing the servants.

ↄ

Poor Mary Chadleigh was long held in ignorance of this, to her, overwhelming catastrophe. At length, however, it could be no longer concealed; and the revelation was followed by a brain-fever, which first threatened her life, and then her reason. She recovered, however, with a mind unimpaired, although with a shattered constitution. With her younger brother and her child, the youthful widow found an asylum for years in England, until the death of Sir Arthur put her in possession of the fortune which his will could not control.

One circumstance connected with the history of Jennings' fate, however, never reached her ear. I had taken care to procure, though not without considerable difficulty at starting, the fullest evidence of the marriage—and afterwards learned, from the younger brother, whose return had, perhaps, precipitated the catastrophe, a circumstance which accounted for what had, for a time, appeared to me the gratuitous villainy of Jennings, in himself denying, and suborning others to deny, a marriage, whose existence was necessary to protect Miss Chadleigh from the agonizing degradation, the appalling ruin, with which she had been so imminently, though unconsciously, threatened. Jennings, it seemed, had actually married a woman of very equivocal rank, and more than equivocal character, in India. There were circumstances, however, which made the validity of this marriage doubtful, and the woman herself had left him, and formed a vicious connexion there; so that he had regarded the marriage as dissolved by mutual consent, and never reckoned upon the remote contingency of her turning up, by any accident. By a fatal coincidence, however, it happened, that, of the few individuals who knew of this connexion, his intimate and confidential friend, Captain Chadleigh, had been one. His supposed death had, however, quieted those alarms, which would have precluded the moral possibility of Jennings' hazarding the audacious step which ended so fatally for himself, and the unexpected and impending return of Chadleigh was the first event which recalled the reckless and unprincipled man to a sense of his actual position. How often is crime unavailing for its meditated purpose, and effective only for the ruin of him who plans it. While Jennings was stoutly denying his marriage with Mary Chadleigh, to avoid the fancied danger of a prosecution, the poor young lady's brother was bringing with him tidings of the death (long previous to his marriage with Miss Chadleigh) of the profligate woman, whose claim upon his hand had driven him to the selfish and desperate expedient of denying his union with the too-confiding creature whom his ardent and impetuous pursuit had won to life-long sorrow. Yet I have lived to see the offspring of this inauspicious marriage, Arthur Chadleigh, a member of parliament, and the sole inheritor of the great Chadleigh estates in Ireland.

From an Ancient, Leathern Armchair: Some Notes on Le Fanu's Bachelor

Jim Rockhill & Brian J. Showers

Since it first saw print over 150 years ago, "The Watcher" has remained one of Joseph Sheridan Le Fanu's best known and most appreciated tales of the uncanny. Set during the foundation of Georgian Dublin and featuring one of Le Fanu's classic doomed protagonists, the tale was recognised by M.R. James as one of the cornerstones of the modern ghost story. "The Watcher" was originally published anonymously in the November 1847 issue of the *Dublin University Magazine*, then edited by James F. Waller. And in a neat moment of literary serendipity, fellow Dubliner and scribe of the gothic, Bram Stoker, was born on the eighth day of that very same month.

"The Watcher" was the first story Le Fanu had published after a four-year absence from the pages of the *DUM*. His output during the 1840s was understandably sparse. The late 1830s saw a three-year burst of creative activity, beginning with "The Ghost and the Bone-Setter" in January 1838; the last of these twelve Purcell Papers, "The Quare Gander", was published in October of 1840. Le Fanu might have continued at this pace, but tragedy struck the household in March 1841 when his sister Catherine passed away, after a long illness, at the age of twenty-seven. The only other story written during these grief-stricken

121

years was a gothic novella of Italian diablerie, "Spalatro" (March/April 1843).

Le Fanu must have greatly appreciated his own masterful story of spectral revenge as he rightly saw fit to include "The Watcher" in his first collection *Ghost Stories and Tales of Mystery* (McGlashan, 1851). Twenty-five years later he still deemed the story worthy enough to re-appropriate for what would become his most celebrated volume, *In a Glass Darkly* (Bentley, 1872)—with an added prologue, textual revisions, and a new title, "The Familiar"—where it joined the ranks of such classics as "Green Tea", "Justice Harbottle", and "Carmilla", thus ensuring that the harrowing tale of Captain Barton, damned and dogged by supernatural agencies, would never be forgotten.

Just over two decades after *In a Glass Darkly* was published, "The Watcher" reappeared as the title story of the posthumous volume *The Watcher and Other Weird Stories* (Downey, 1894), selected and illustrated by the author's son Brinsley. The book's cover bears a memorable illustration stamped onto its grey, cloth boards: an infernal owl with its wings stretched out across a cloudy and moonlit sky. Among those possessing a copy of this attractive volume was Bram Stoker, whose auction catalogue upon his death listed this book as one of the titles in his personal library.

Although Le Fanu and posterity recognised the merits of "The Watcher", and ensured its survival beyond the pages of the *Dublin University Magazine*, its companion piece "The Fatal Bride" has been virtually forgotten, languishing out of print since its initial publication in the January 1848 issue of the *DUM*. The present collection sees not only "The Fatal Bride" reprinted for the first time in over 150 years, but also published alongside "The Watcher", as per the author's initial intention.

Though the two narratives read as unconnected stories, they were originally unified by their subtitles: "The Watcher" bore the description "From the Reminiscences of a Bachelor", while "The Fatal Bride" was published as "Being a Second Contribution from the Reminiscences of a Bachelor". There would be no third reminiscence. Le Fanu's next contribution to the *DUM* was a standalone mystery tale with no sub-attribution: "Some Account of the Latter Days of Richard Marston, of Dunoran" (April - June 1848). Interestingly, Le Fanu chose to place "Richard Marston" (with its new title "The Evil Guest") alongside "The Watcher" in *Ghost Stories and Tales of Mystery*, stranding "The Fatal Bride" within the yellowing pages of the *DUM*. Exactly why Le Fanu did this, or indeed why he abandoned the "Bachelor" persona after only two installments, is unknown. Perhaps the Bachelor's flickering candle had at last gone out? However, this was neither Le Fanu's first use of a serial narrator, nor would it be his last.

Le Fanu used the literary device of the serial narrator throughout his career. This device was neither unusual nor particularly innovative, and was widely used in the fiction magazines of the day. Indeed, Samuel Warren's *Passages from the Diary of a Late Physician*, which was serialised in *Blackwood's Magazine* between 1832 and 1837, may have served as a possible inspiration for Dr. Martin Hesselius, whose papers are ostensibly collected between the covers of *In a Glass Darkly*. Le Fanu's Bachelor is in august company.

As mentioned earlier, Le Fanu's first eleven stories (and one mock essay) appeared in the *Dublin University Magazine* between January 1838 and October 1840 as extracts "from the MS. Papers of the Late Rev. Francis Purcell, of Drumcoolagh". They were collected posthumously as *The Purcell Papers* in 1880. These early tales already reveal characteristics, such as the serialised narrator, found in

123

later series like *Chronicles of Golden Friars* (serialised between 1869 and 1871 before book publication in 1871), *In a Glass Darkly* (serialised in various magazines between 1847 and 1872), and the episodic novel *The House by the Church-yard* (cast in the serialised text as nostalgic ruminations "By Charles de Cresseron"; *DUM*, October 1861 - February, 1863; Tinsley Brothers, 1863). Even the aforementioned "Spalatro", though a novella in two parts, purports to be "From the Notes of Fra. Giacomo".

With perhaps the exception of *Golden Friars*, which uses a fictional village to link its three tales, each series has its own narrator-persona. Yet they all share common traits. There is frequently a sense of wistfulness about absent friends, lost innocence, missed opportunities, and vanished ways of life in these stories, told from the vantage point of reminiscences recovered from the papers of the dead, the aged, or the infirm. Events range from those recent and directly observed to those involving a number of auxiliary narrators recalling scenes from a more remote location or more distant past. The two stories that comprise *Reminiscences of a Bachelor* are no different. In fact, the Bachelor may be seen as an early adumbration in tone, attitude, and age to the curious fellow who narrates *The House by the Church-yard*, whose name bears the autobiographical distinction of resembling the author's seventeenth century ancestor, Charles Le Fanu de Cresserons, who had served under William III at the Battle of the Boyne.

It is also notable that, while "The Watcher" is a tale of the supernatural, "The Fatal Bride", though similar in its use of brooding gothic suspense, is a story without flourishes of the fantastic. This aesthetic incongruity may draw criticism from modern readers, but for Le Fanu and regular readers of the *DUM* such practice was common.

Perhaps taking his cue from books such as Irving's *The Sketch Book of Geoffrey Crayon, Gent.* (1819), Hawthorne's *Twice-Told Tales* (1837-42), Barham's *The Ingoldsby Legends* (1840-47), or Poe's *Tales of the Grotesque and Arabesque* (1840), Le Fanu freely mingled tales of the supernatural with their less fanciful, though no less suspenseful counterparts. His panoramic chronicle of village life, *The House by the Church-yard*, sports two chapters devoted to "Ghost Stories of the Tiled House"; the sombre *Guy Deverell* (1865) introduces a fragmentary vampire story to symbolise one of the situations in a plot otherwise resembling the mysteries of Wilkie Collins; and *In a Glass Darkly* opens with three ghost stories in succession before offering the non-supernatural adventure story "The Room in the Dragon Volant" as a bit of a palate cleanser prior to "Carmilla". Even the title Le Fanu gave to his debut collection, *Ghost Stories and Tales of Mystery*, plainly represents two sides of the same coin: the irrational and the rational.

One advantage of this arrangement is that the supernatural can be seen to emerge just as naturally from the carefully described settings as do the events that unfold in the less fanciful tales. This not only lends an additional touch of hushed expectancy to the more mundane events, but also lulls the reader into a false sense of familiarity and security, which succeeds in making the advent of the uncanny even more unsettling. To quote M.R. James, who codified Le Fanu's technique in his introduction to *Ghosts & Marvels* (1924):

> Let us, then, be introduced to the actors in a placid way; let us see them going about their ordinary business, undisturbed by forebodings, pleased with their surroundings; and into this calm environment let the ominous thing put out its head, unobtru-

sively at first, and then more insistently, until it holds the stage.

There is a balance at work here, between the fantastic and consensus reality, which twenty-first century readers used to reading magazines and books clearly marketed for any one of a variety of different genres may not be accustomed to encountering. Le Fanu embraces that balance, as he had throughout his life as a writer, creating two matched stories, which offer complementary views of Dublin from opposite sides of reality. The events in "The Fatal Bride" take place along the same streets described in "The Watcher" after all, its characters' steps falling alongside those of its predecessor. Perhaps that is why he felt no need to continue the series.

Texts for both "The Watcher" and "The Fatal Bride" have been taken from their original appearances in the *Dublin University Magazine*. While there is no other version of "The Fatal Bride", "The Watcher" was slightly revised by Le Fanu for its inclusion in *Ghost Stories and Tales of Mystery* in 1851 and has since become the preferred version of the story under that title.

Finally, and before anyone accuses the editors of this book of violence against Le Fanu's writing, we would like to admit that one alteration has been made to the original text: the addition of the "Prologue". Please note that the paragraphs used for the "Prologue" of this edition were originally the opening paragraphs of "The Fatal Bride". As no similar introductory lines had been written for "The Watcher", and because we feel these paragraphs give more context to both of the Bachelor's reminiscences, we decided to appropriate these for the "Prologue". Nothing else has been altered or changed, save for the occasional typographical error that appeared in the original text, or where the slightest alteration of grammar makes a sentence substantially clearer. We do feel, though, that the addition of the "Prologue" is in keeping with Le Fanu's own authorial habits. Not only did he frequently revise stories for their inclusion in collections, but he often added prologues so the tales would read better as a unified work. In any case, we hope both readers of the present volume and the author himself, wherever his spirit might be, will kindly forgive us this editorial decision and look upon our efforts with favour.

Some Notes on "The Watcher"

Jim Rockhill & Brian J. Showers

The transformation of "The Watcher" (1847) into "The Familiar" (1872) is marked by a number of divagations and reconsiderations. While these edits leave most of the story unchanged, they do alter details and subtle emphases worth considering more closely. Like the Bachelor himself, we shall attempt in the following pages, however imperfectly, to illuminate the darkness which involves the progress and termination of Le Fanu's classic story.

There are three distinct variations of "The Watcher". All three were published during Le Fanu's lifetime (1814-1873), and therefore all edits and revisions were likely done with his knowledge, if not direct involvement. The first version of "The Watcher" appeared in the *Dublin University Magazine* in November 1847. The second version of the text, also titled "The Watcher", was collected in *Ghost Stories and Tales of Mystery* issued by the *DUM*'s publisher James McGlashan in 1851. The third and final iteration of the tale was given a new title: "The Familiar", and appeared in *In a Glass Darkly* (1872). When "The Watcher" was posthumously reprinted in *The Watcher and Other Weird Stories* (Downey, 1894), the text was taken from *Ghost Stories and Tales of Mystery*, probably with the assumption that this latest version was the author's preferred text. The 1851 version of "The Watcher"

"

has since become the standard text for subsequent re-printing under that title.

The text used in the present edition is from the story's first appearance in the *Dublin University Magazine* (1847), a version not reprinted since that time.

Of the three iterations, the differences between "The Watcher" (1851) and "The Familiar" (1872) have been given the most attention. This is due in part to the enduring reputation of the volume for which Le Fanu revised the latter version. Published in December 1872, *In a Glass Darkly* purports to be a collection of five case-notes from the files of German metaphysical physician Doctor Martin Hesselius— "The Familiar" is one of those cases. The other four stories in the collection, all of which had been previously published, were also revised and given prologues so as to become part of the collection's case-book framework.

One notable addition found only in the 1851 version of "The Watcher" is an epigraph from the Book of Job: "How long wilt thou not depart from me? Thou terrifiest me through visions: so that my soul chooseth strangling rather than my life" (Chapter 7, Verses 14-15). Le Fanu added Bible verses to two of the other three stories that appeared in *Ghost Stories and Tales of Mystery*: "Schalken the Painter" and "The Murdered Cousin"; "The Evil Guest" appeared without an epigraph. When Le Fanu revised the title again for *In a Glass Darkly* in 1872, the Bible verse was omitted and the title was changed from "The Watcher" to "The Familiar". The effect of these additional edits subtly shifted attention away from the supernatural threat as a visitation inflicted upon Captain Barton from outside to a focus that stresses the relationship between external phenomena and their roots within Captain Barton's personality and past behaviour. This is thematically consistent with most of the other stories from *In a Glass Darkly*.

Nor did the openings of each version escape Le Fanu's editorial pen. While "The Familiar" dispenses with the first paragraph common to both earlier versions of the tale, Le Fanu reinstated the second paragraph of the 1847 text to the final version of the story without changing a single word ("I was a young man at the time . . . "). This second paragraph is entirely absent from the 1851 version. The reason for this excision is unclear, though perhaps Le Fanu, for *Ghost Stories and Tales of Mystery*—a collection of unrelated tales without a serial narrator—did not want to stress the first person narrator asserted in the 1847 text. This greater intimacy of narration was reasserted in "The Familiar", possibly to establish the credentials of Doctor Hesselius's central narrator.

This restoration of "The Familiar" to the 1847 text's sense of intimacy recurs at intervals throughout the story, frequently reinstating the first person "I" which had been replaced by "they" in 1851. As discussed earlier, "The Familiar" rests in a framing narrative as one of Doctor Hesselius's case-studies. Like its companions in *In a Glass Darkly*, Le Fanu divided "The Familiar" into chapters, also breaking up the longer paragraphs into shorter ones. Additionally, unique to "The Familiar", we are told in the "Prologue" that the story itself is the "Narrative of the Rev. Thomas Herbert", whereas the narrator of the 1847 text is the Bachelor. Their roles, nonetheless, are practically identical, eyewitnesses to events that had been rendered in the third person in the story's intermediate 1851 version. However, in "The Familiar" the Rev. Thomas Herbert, like the Bachelor, is directly involved in the story. In the 1847 text, the early scene in which Captain Barton is walking down to the House of Commons with his companions before first hearing and then encountering his spectral nemesis is virtually identical to the end of Chapter II and beginning of

Chapter III of "The Familiar". But in the 1851 revision, Le Fanu re-attributed some of the Bachelor's (and Rev. Thomas Herbert's) direct experiences to a character named Norcott. While the character of Norcott does participate in the other two versions, his role is not only reduced, but he is referred to anonymously with two em-dashes.

This reduction of character names to initials or dashes was a common feature in the fiction of Le Fanu's predecessors and contemporaries, whose modern equivalent is perhaps the disclaimer common to televised crime dramas in which "The story you are about to hear is true; only the names have been changed to protect the innocent". As a stand-alone story in *Ghost Stories and Tales of Mystery*, Le Fanu was less concerned with reinforcing the verisimilitude of the events he narrates by changing or altering the names of participants than he was in either of the other two versions; thus "——" becomes "Norcott", "Lady L——" becomes "Lady Rochdale", "Dr. R——", becomes "Dr. Richards"; and "Doctor ——" becomes "Doctor Macklin" for the 1851 text alone, before reverting back to their disguised forms for "The Familiar" in 1872.

Another feature of the 1847 text is Le Fanu's extensive use of em-dashes—in the 1851 version many of these have been replaced with commas and semi-colons, either by Le Fanu or more likely by McGlashan's copyeditor. Furthermore, a handful of commas had been added, while others were deleted. Although none of these affect the narrative itself, in several places they do improve the flow of the sentence, and were maintained for *In a Glass Darkly*.

No version of "The Watcher" is considered superior to the others. Indeed, Le Fanu had tailored each version to fit perfectly within the context of each publication. Indeed, when putting together their three-volume edition of Le Fanu's *Collected Supernatural Stories*, Ash-Tree Press felt

"The Watcher" (1851) and "The Familiar" (1872), were sufficiently different from one another to warrant the inclusion of both.

Now, "The Watcher", along with its companion "The Fatal Bride", appear together again between two covers. And we have also used this occasion to further celebrate the bicentenary of the author's birth by reprinting "The Watcher" as it originally appeared in the *Dublin University Magazine* over a century and a half ago.

Acknowledgements

The editors would like to thank all those who helped
in the preparation of this volume, including
Matthew Holness, Meggan Kehrli, Paul Lowe,
Ken Mackenzie, Terri Neil, Jim Rockhill,
Olga Taranova, and the Le Fanu Family.

"The Watcher"
first appeared in the
Dublin University Magazine, November 1847.
It was first collected in *Ghost Stories and
Tales of Mystery* (Dublin: McGlashan, 1851).

"The Fatal Bride"
first appeared in the
Dublin University Magazine, January 1848.
It is reprinted here for the first time.

About the Author

About the Author

Joseph Sheridan Le Fanu was born in Dublin on 28 August 1814. Though he worked as a journalist and owned several newspapers, he is now best remembered for his pioneering tales of the psychological and supernatural such as "Schalken the Painter", "Green Tea", and "Carmilla". His notable novels include *The House by the Churchyard* (1863) and *Uncle Silas* (1864). Le Fanu's seminal short story collection *In a Glass Darkly* was published in 1872, less than a year before his death on 7 February 1873.

SWAN RIVER PRESS

Founded in 2003, Swan River Press is an independent publishing company, based in Dublin, Ireland, dedicated to gothic, supernatural, and fantastic literature. We specialise in limited edition hardbacks, publishing fiction from around the world with an emphasis on Ireland's contributions to the genre.

www.swanriverpress.ie

*"Handsome, beautifully made volumes . . .
altogether irresistible."*

– Michael Dirda, *Washington Post*

*"It [is] often down to small, independent, specialist presses
to keep the candle of horror fiction flickering . . . "*

– Darryl Jones, *Irish Times*

*"Swan River Press has emerged as one of the most inspiring
new presses over the past decade. Not only are the books
beautifully presented and professionally produced, but they
aspire consistently to high literary quality and originality,
ranging from current writers of supernatural/weird fiction
to rare or forgotten works by departed authors."*

– Peter Bell, *Ghosts & Scholars*

GREEN TEA

J. Sheridan Le Fanu

Published alongside "Carmilla" in the landmark collection *In a Glass Darkly* (1872), Le Fanu's "Green Tea" was first serialised in Charles Dickens' magazine *All the Year Round* in 1869. Since its first publication, Le Fanu's tale has lost none of its potency. "Green Tea" tells of the good natured Reverend Jennings, who writes late at night on arcane topics abetted by a steady supply of green tea. Is he insane or have these nocturnal activities opened an "interior sight" that affords a route of entry for an increasingly malignant simian companion? This 150th anniversary edition of "Green Tea", with illustrations by Alisdair Wood and an introduction by Matthew Holness, is the definitive celebration of Le Fanu's masterpiece of psychological terror and despair.

"Even 150 years after it was published,
'Green Tea' has stood firmly against the test of time
as a wonderfully eerie and well-crafted ghost story."

– Ghosts & Scholars

"To paraphrase Little Women, it wouldn't be Christmas
without any ghost stories . . . Swan River Press
has just issued a beautiful keepsake volume
of J. Sheridan Le Fanu's Green Tea."

– Michael Dirda, *Washington Post*

BENDING TO EARTH
Strange Stories by Irish Women

edited by Maria Giakaniki
and Brian J. Showers

Irish women have long produced literature of the gothic, uncanny, and supernatural. *Bending to Earth* draws together twelve such tales. While none of the authors herein were considered primarily writers of fantastical fiction during their lifetimes, they each wandered at some point in their careers into more speculative realms—some only briefly, others for lengthier stays.

Names such as Charlotte Riddell and Rosa Mulholland will already be familiar to aficionados of the eerie, while Katharine Tynan and Clotilde Graves are sure to gain new admirers. From a ghost story in the Swiss Alps to a premonition of death in the West of Ireland to strange rites in a South Pacific jungle, *Bending to Earth* showcases a diverse range of imaginative writing which spans the better part of a century.

"Bending to Earth *is full of tales of women walled-up in rooms, of vengeful or unforgetting dead wives, of mistreated lovers, of cruel and murderous husbands.*"

– Darryl Jones, *Irish Times*

"*A surprising, extraordinary anthology featuring twelve uncanny and supernatural stories from the nineteenth century . . . highly recommended, extremely enjoyable.*"

– *British Fantasy Society*

GHOSTS OF THE CHIT-CHAT

edited by Robert Lloyd Parry

On the evening of Saturday, 28 October 1893, Cambridge University's Chit-Chat Club convened its 601st meeting. Ten members and one guest gathered in the rooms of Montague Rhodes James, the Junior Dean of King's College, and listened—with increasing absorption one suspects—as their host read "Two Ghost Stories".

Ghosts of the Chit-Chat celebrates this momentous event in the history of supernatural literature, the earliest dated record we have of M. R. James reading his ghost stories out loud. And it revives the contributions that other members made to the genre; men of imagination who invoked the ghostly in their work, and who are now themselves shades. In a series of essays, stories, and poems Robert Lloyd Parry looks at the history and culture of the Club.

In addition to tales and poems never before reprinted, *Ghosts of the Chit-Chat* features earlier, slightly different versions of two of M. R. James's best-known ghost stories; Robert Lloyd Parry's profiles and commentaries on each featured Chit-Chat member sheds new light on this supernatural tradition, making *Ghosts of the Chit-Chat* a valuable resource for casual readers and long-time Jamesians alike.

"An exquisite reading pleasure."

– Black Gate

"This is a lovely little book . . . there are some fascinating and often rarely seen pieces of writing here."

– A Ghostly Company